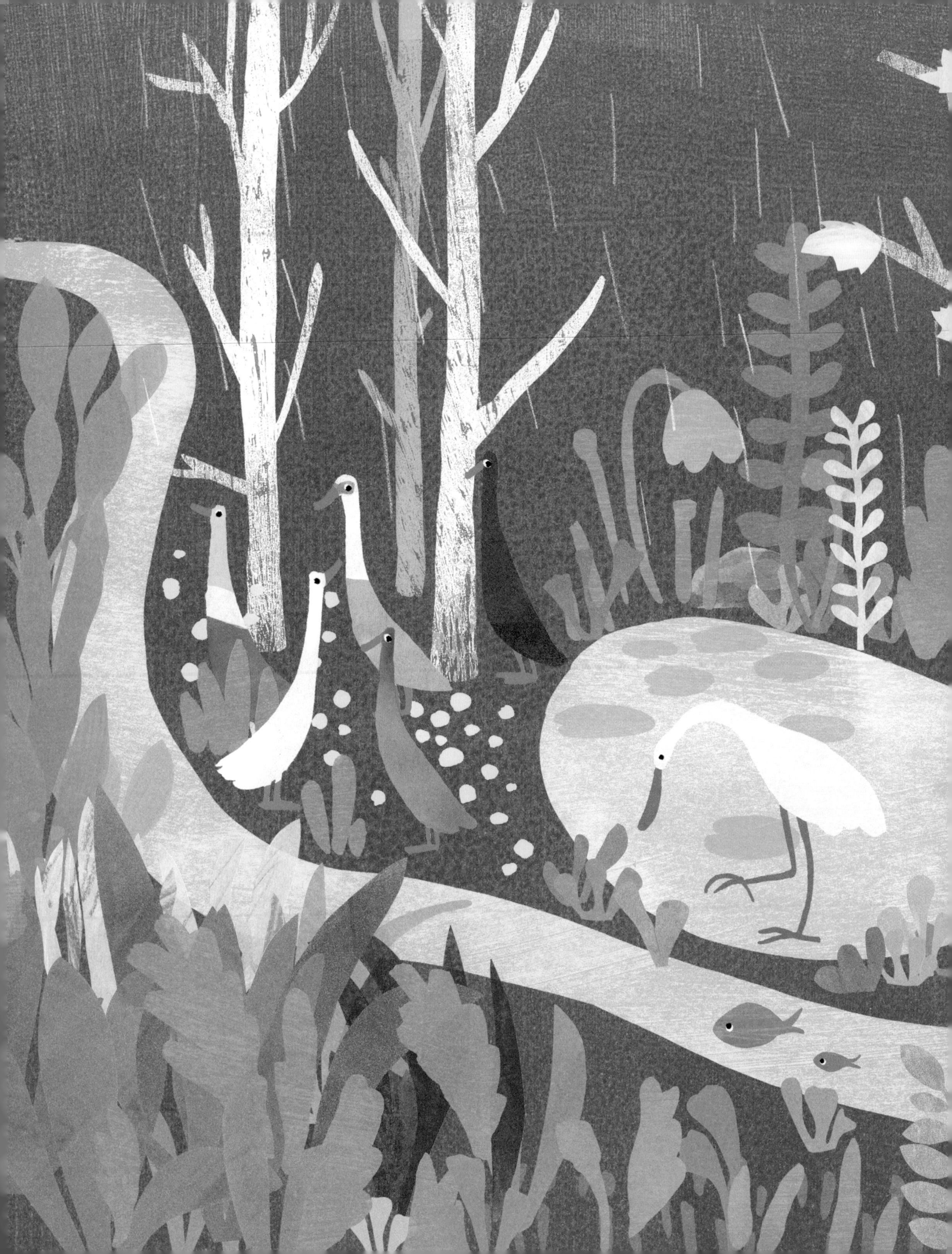

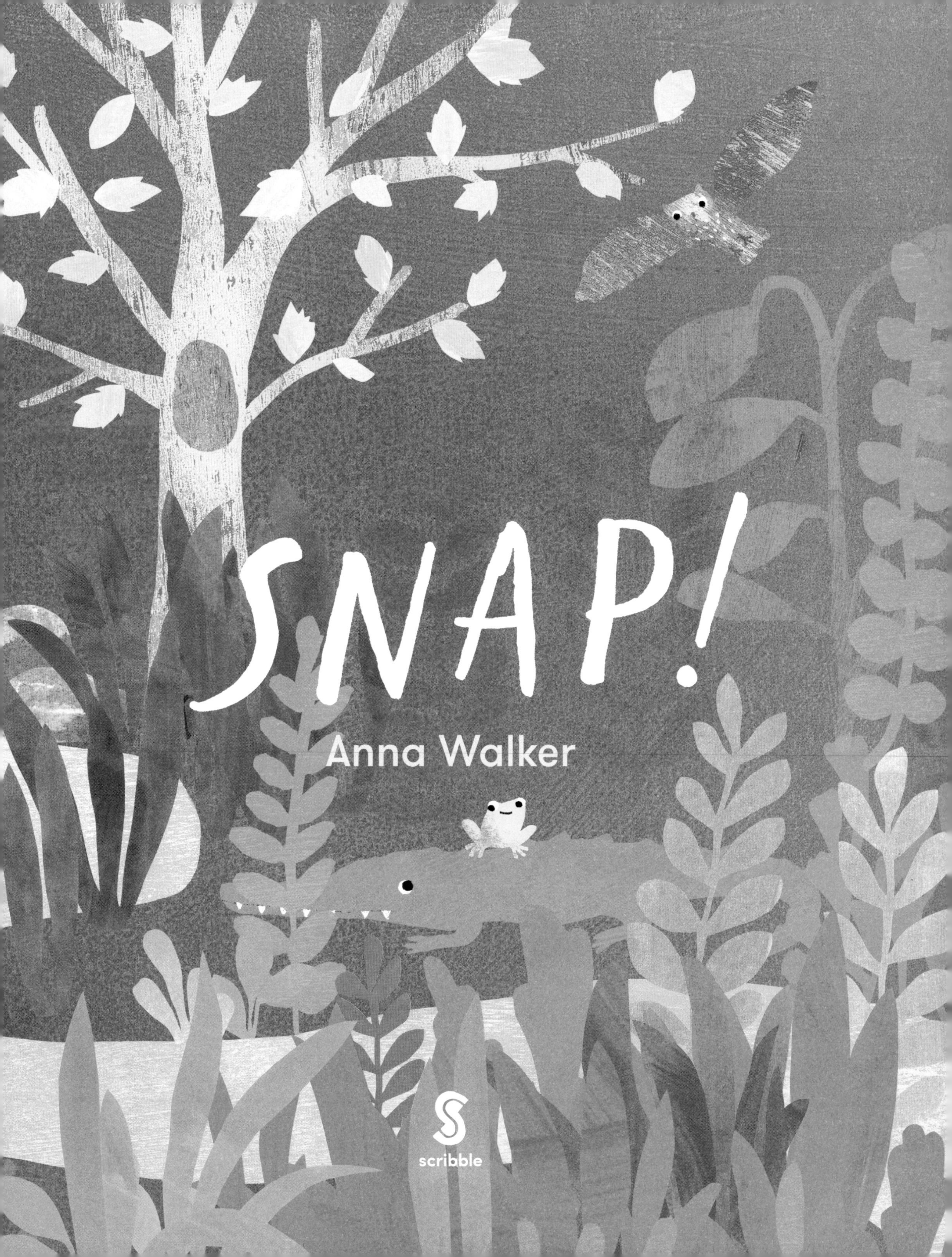
SNAP!
Anna Walker
scribble

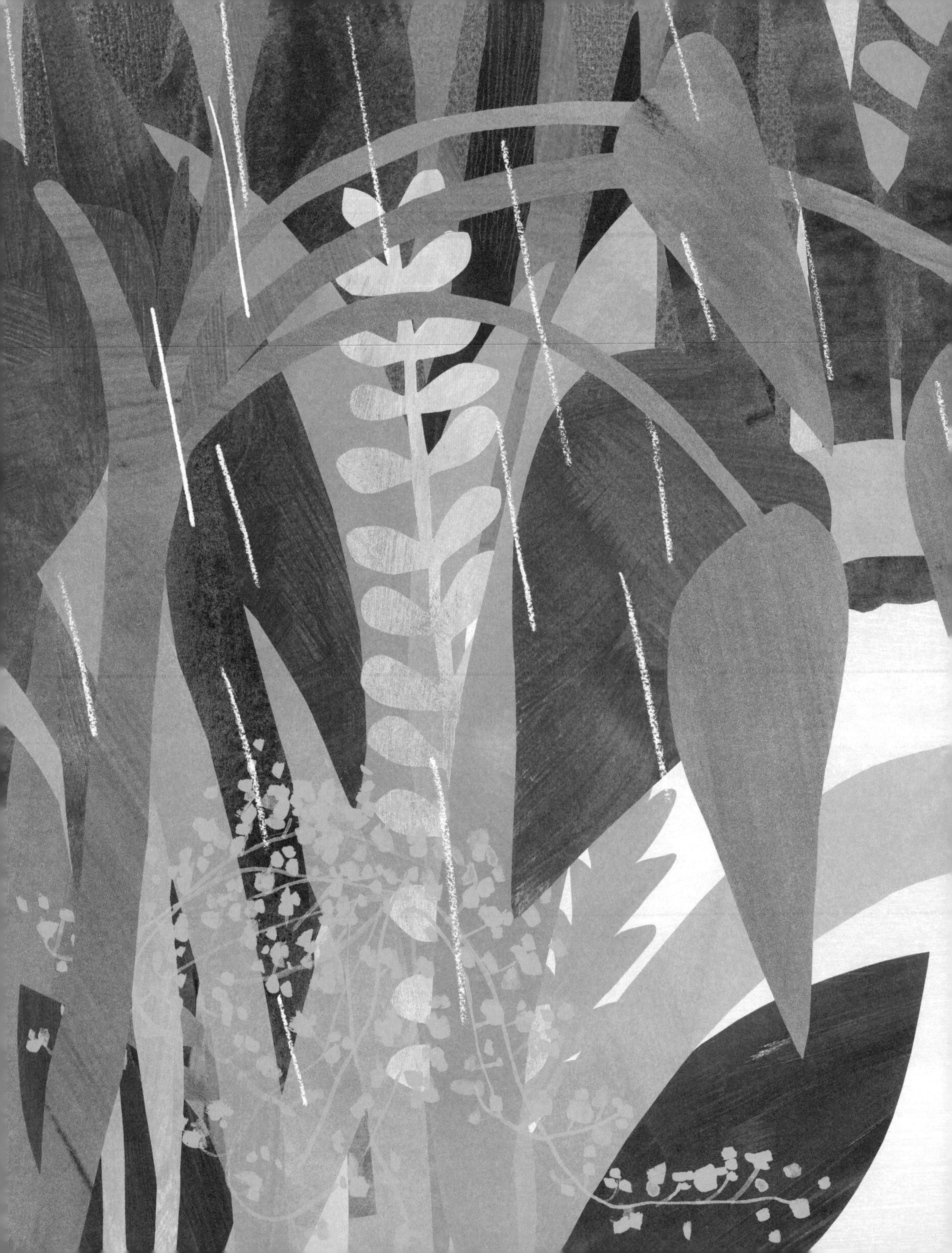

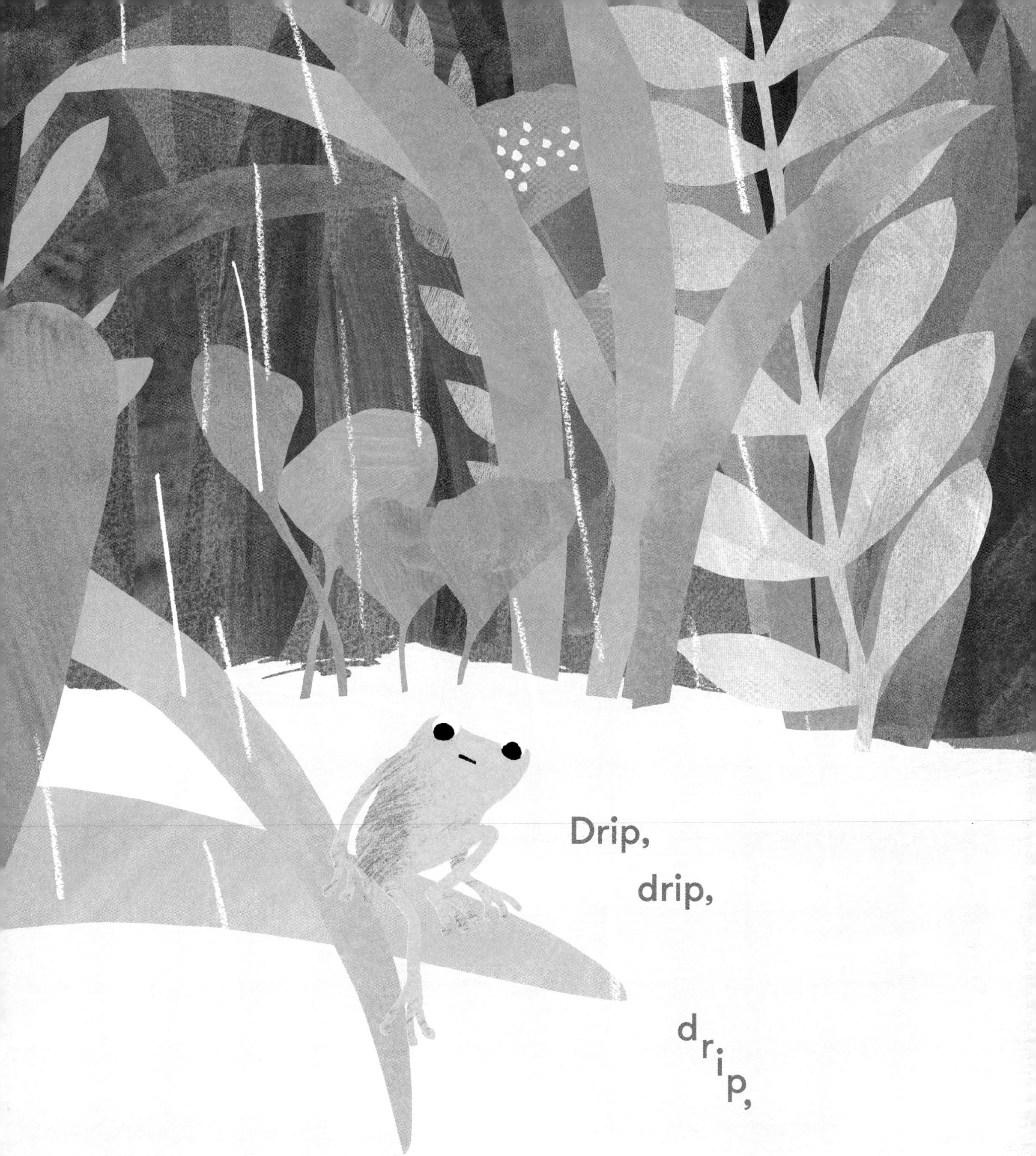

Drip,

drip,

drip,

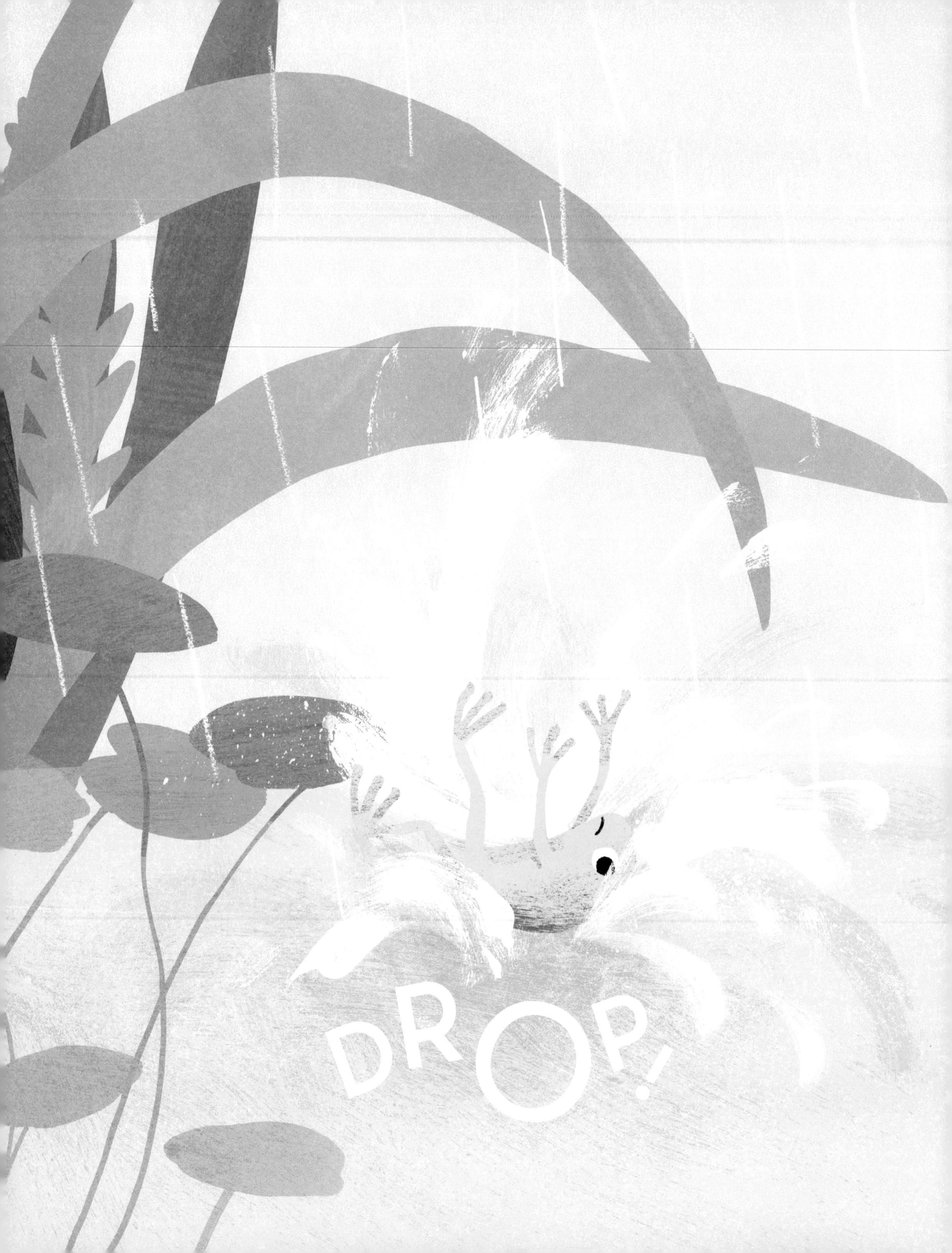
DROP!

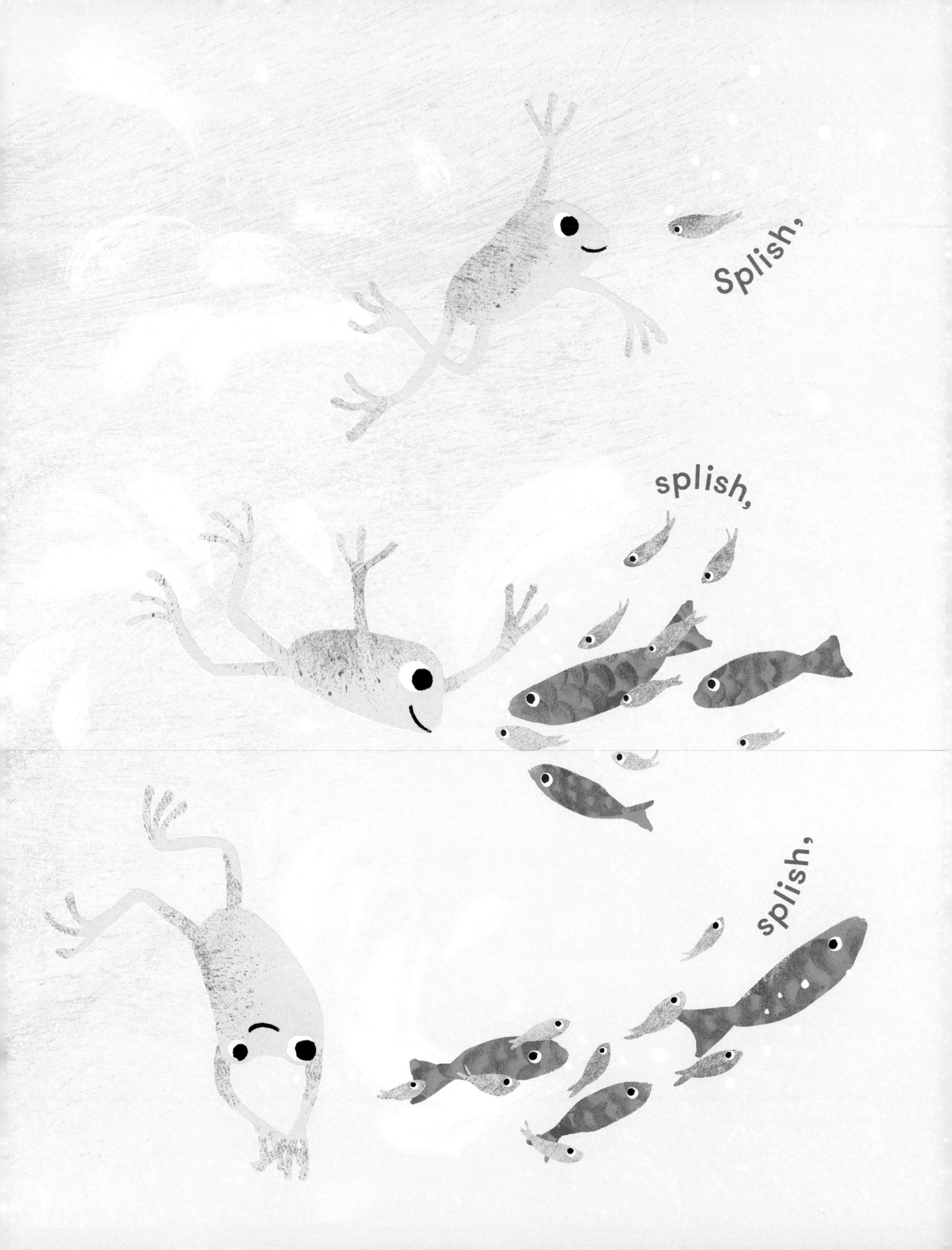

Splish,

splish,

splish,

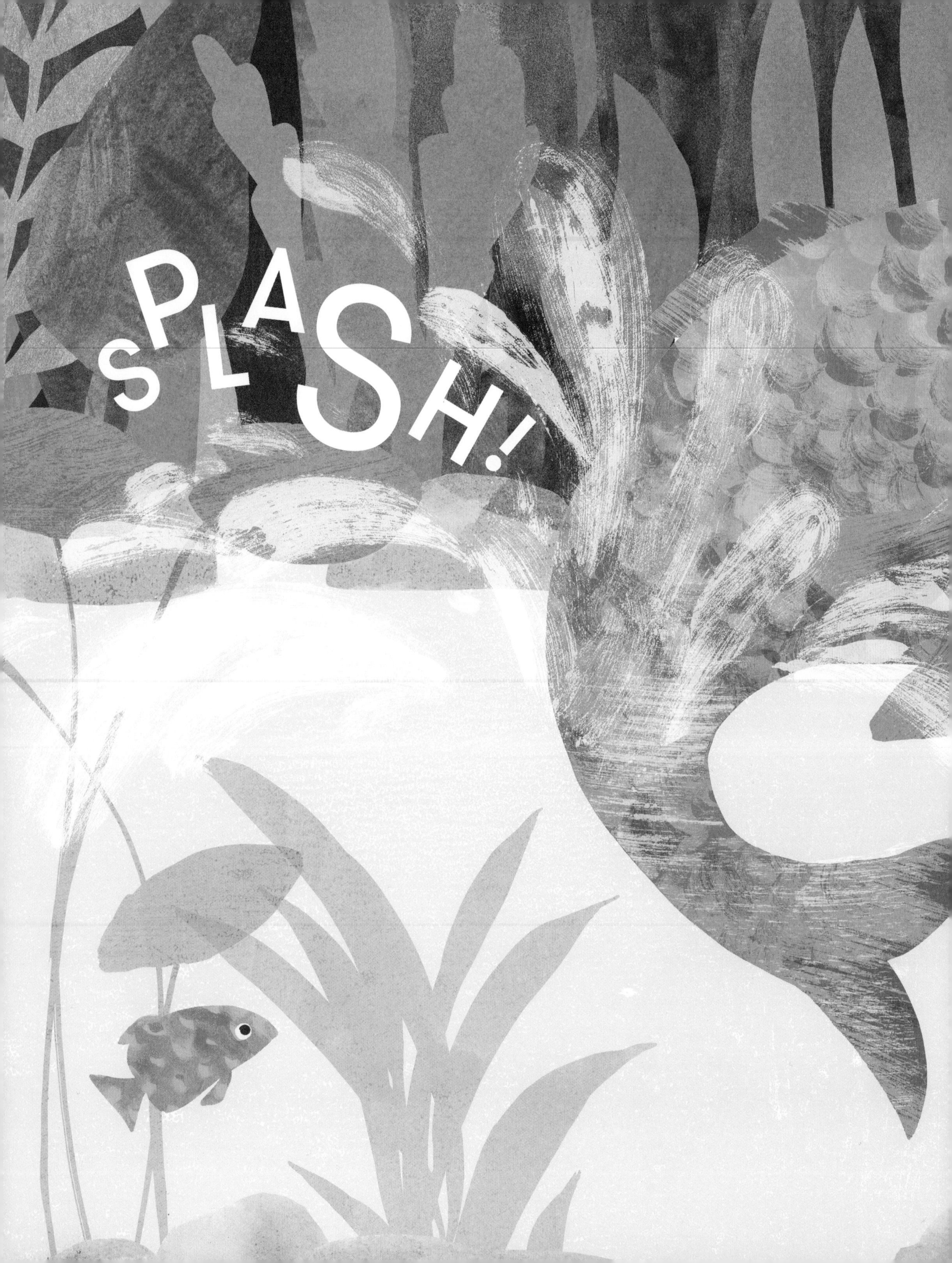
SPLASH!

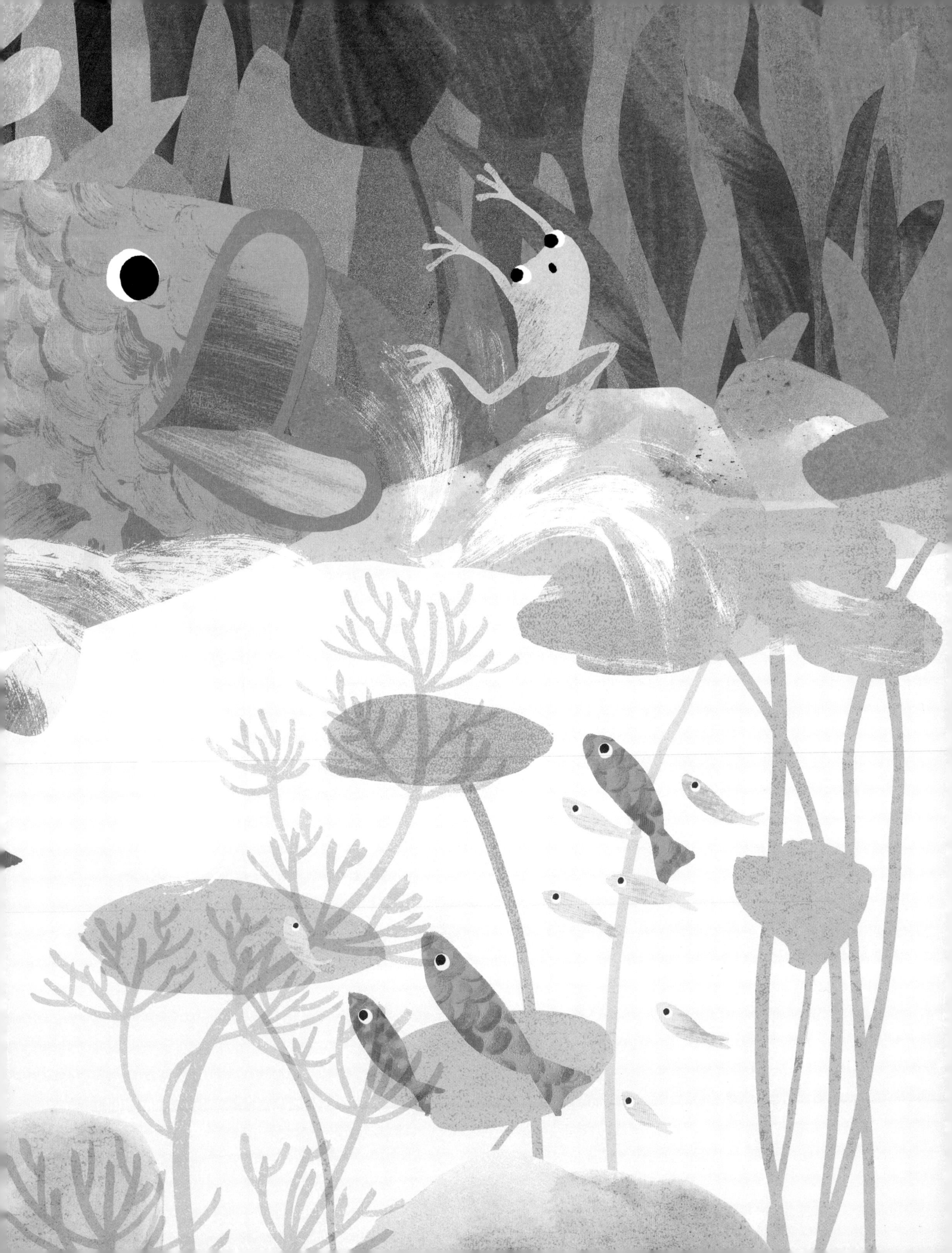

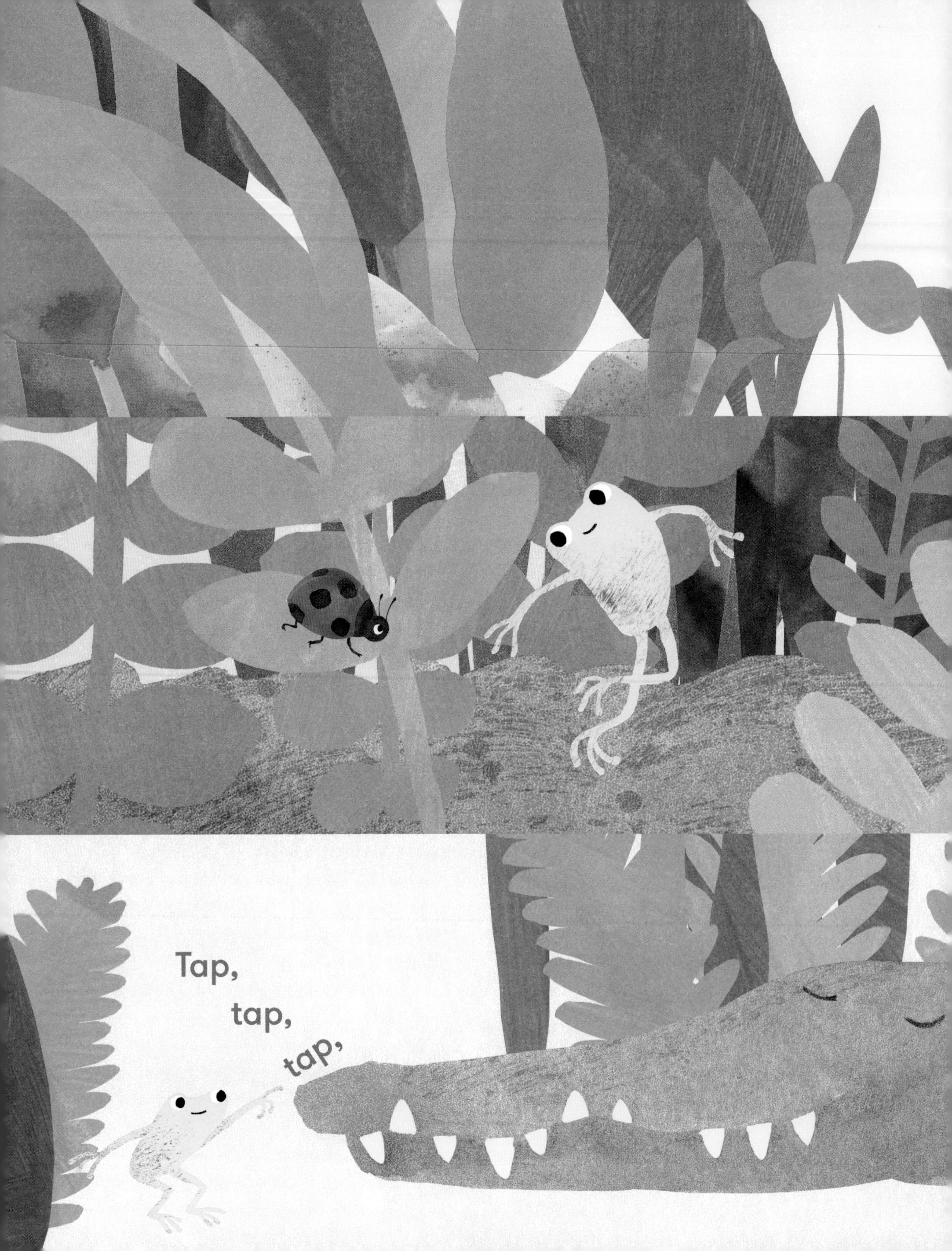
Tap,
tap,
tap,

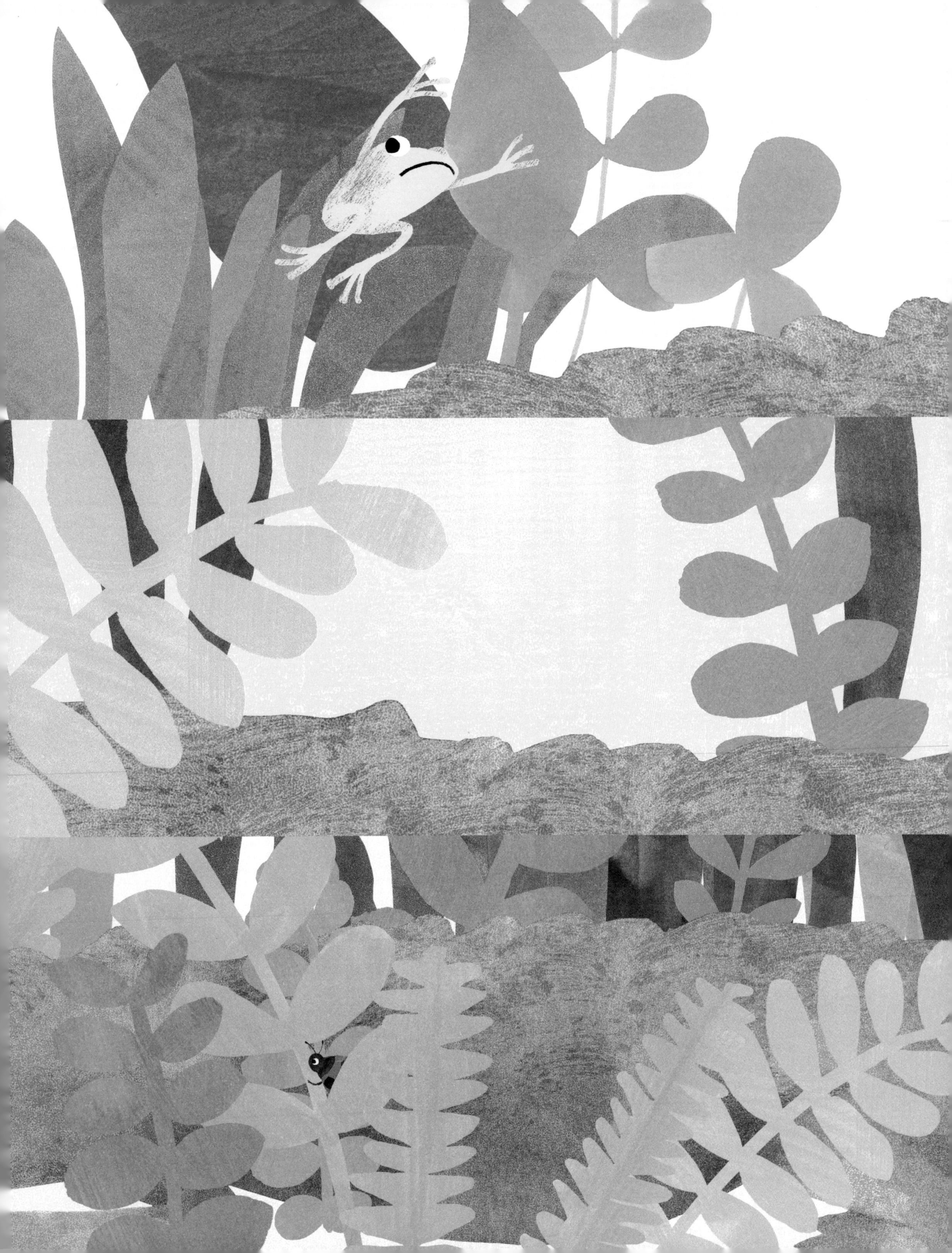

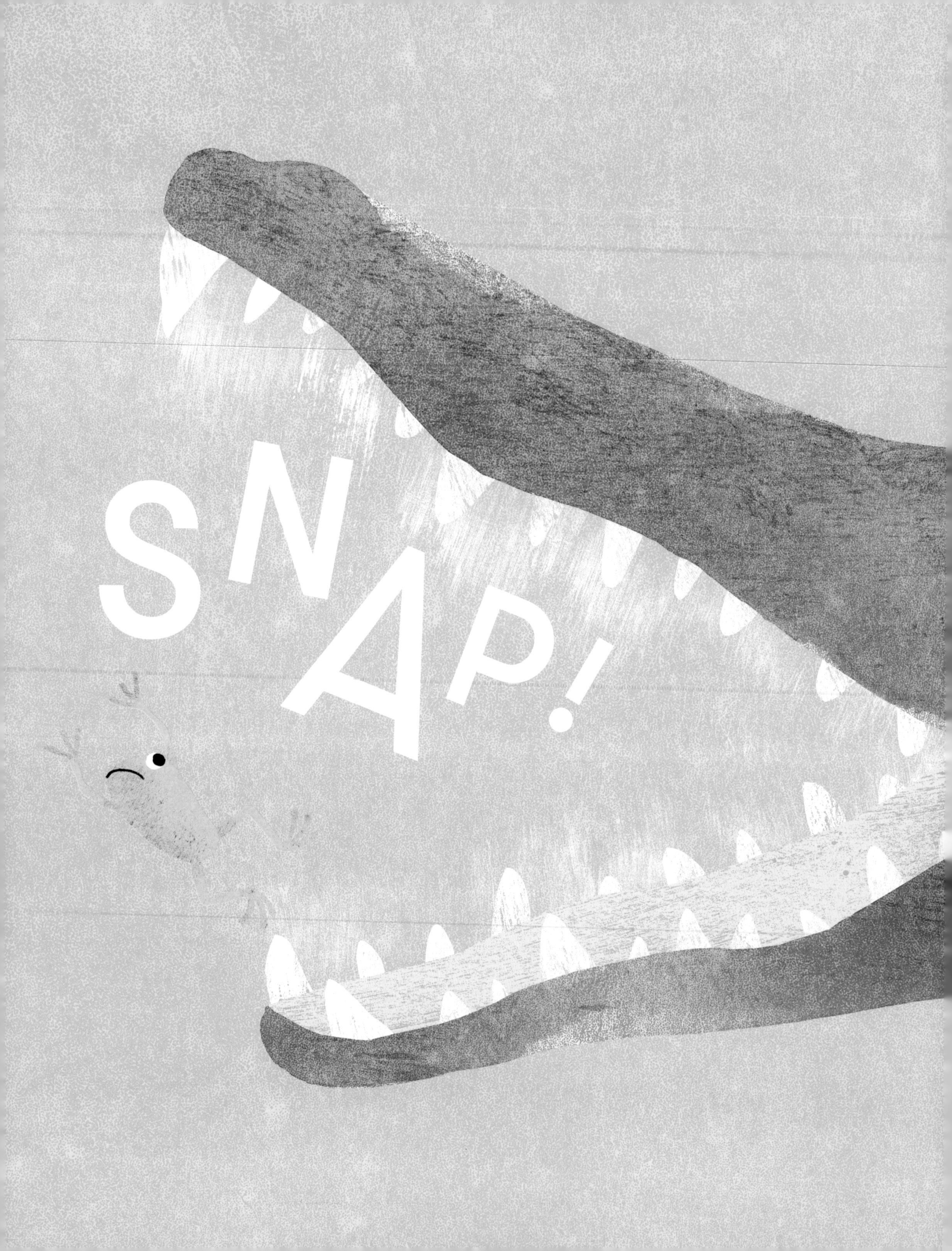
SNAP!

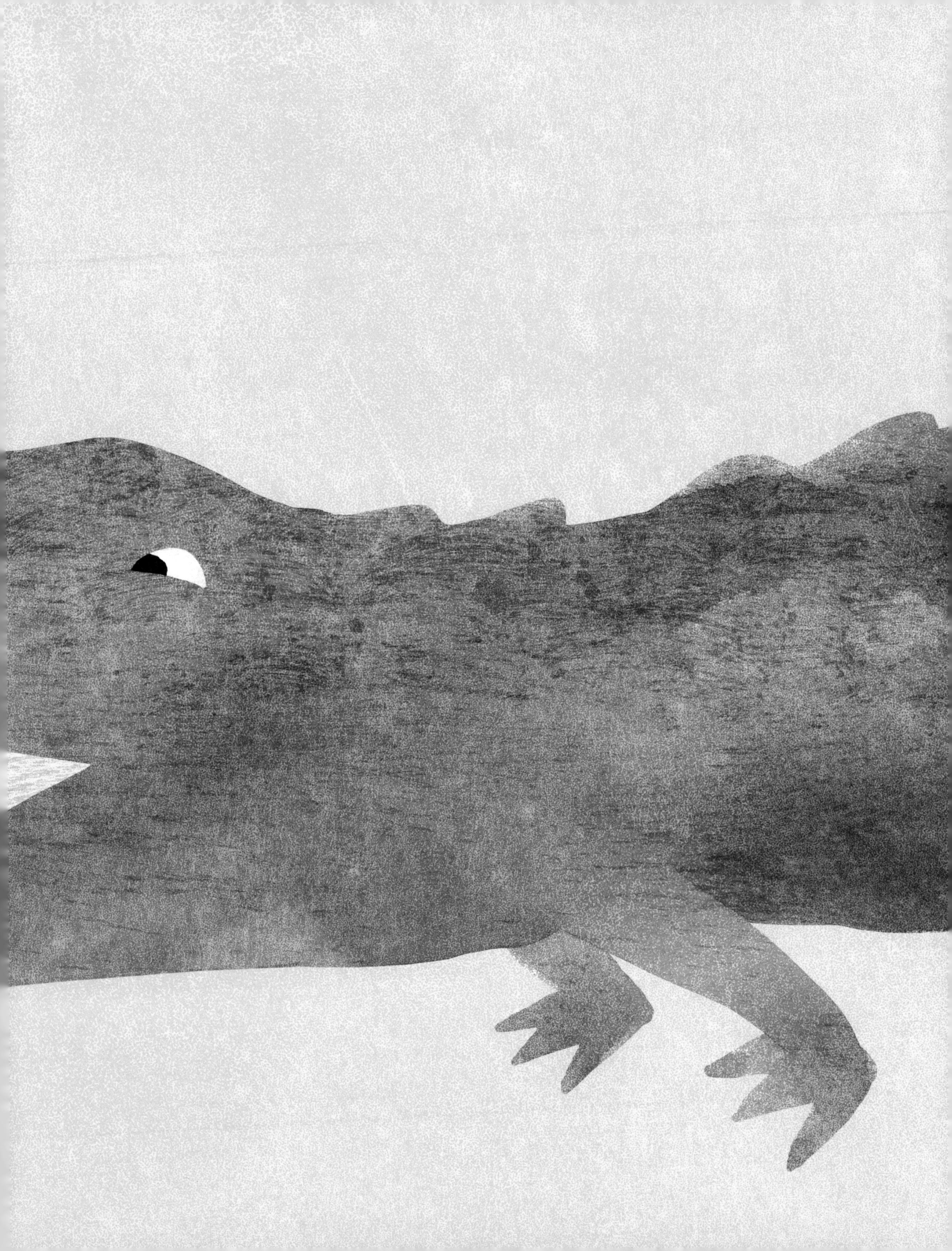

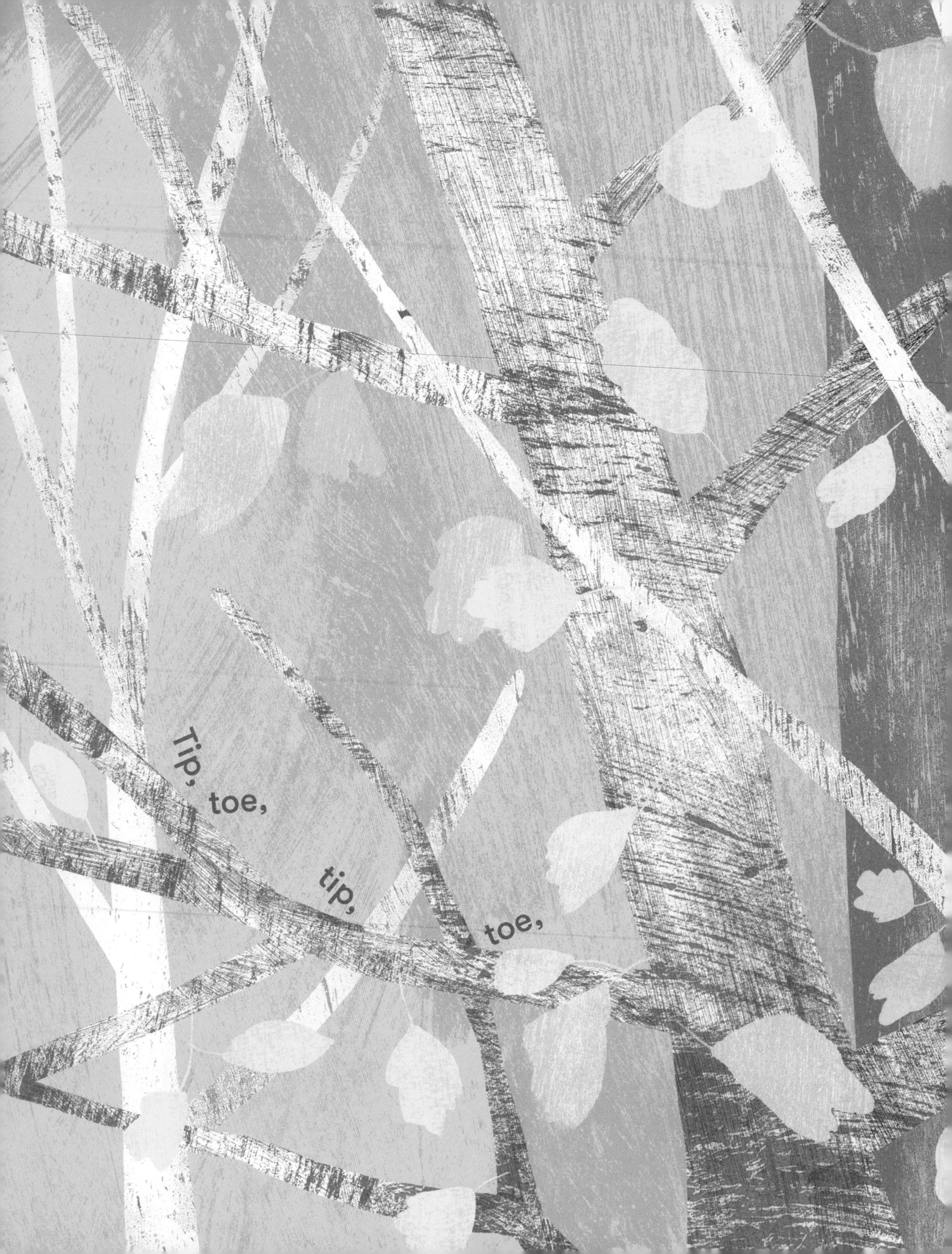

Tip, toe, tip, toe,

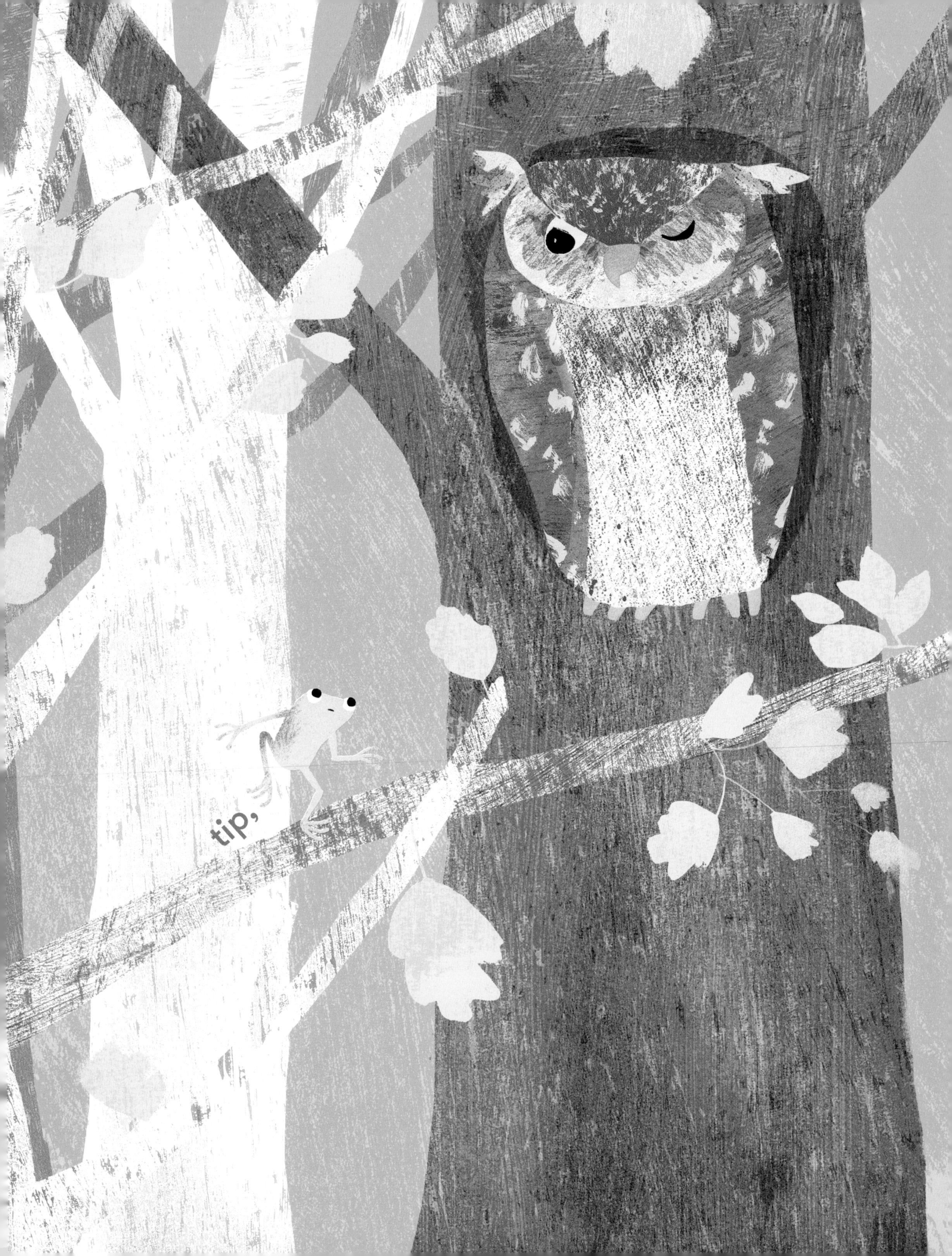
tip,

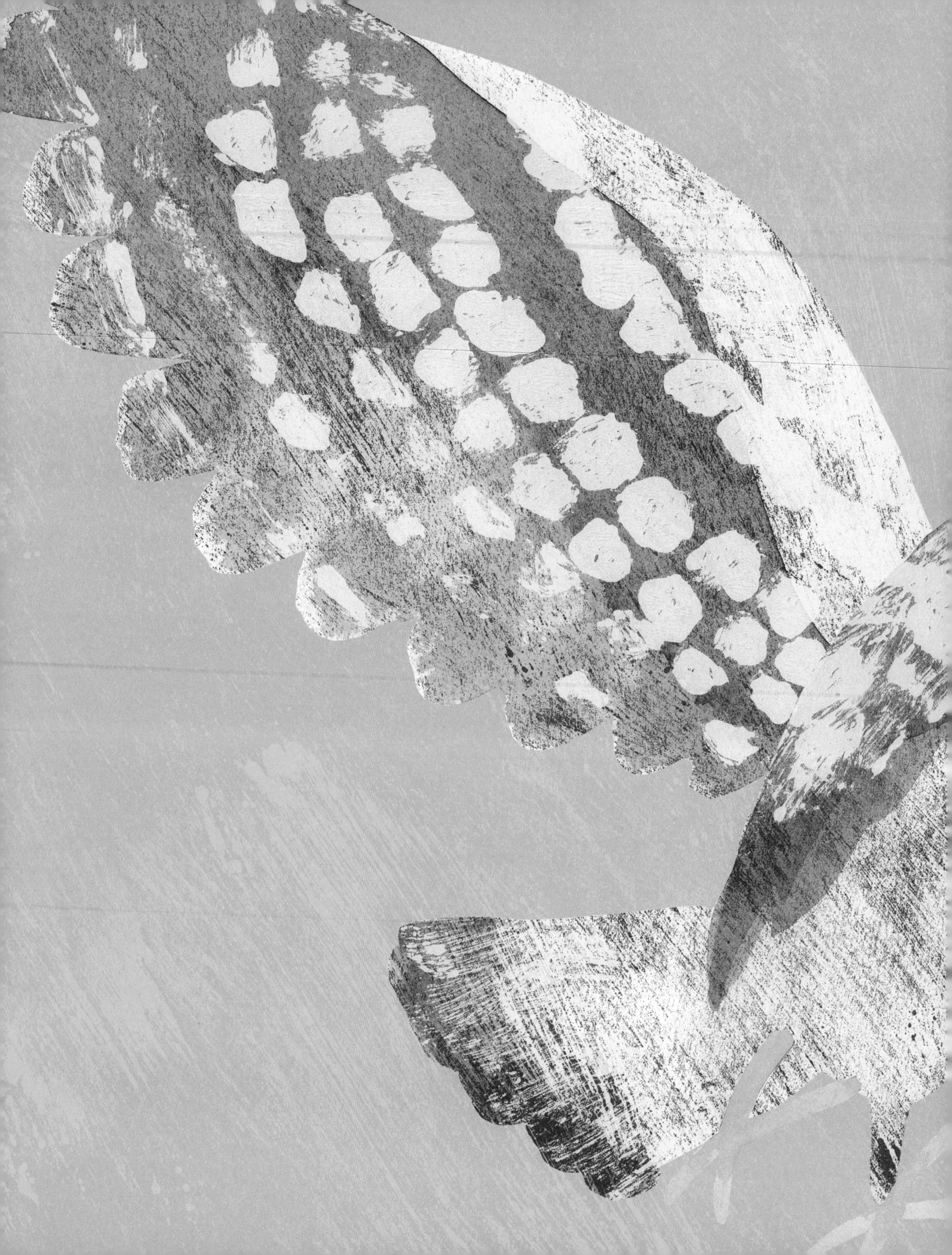

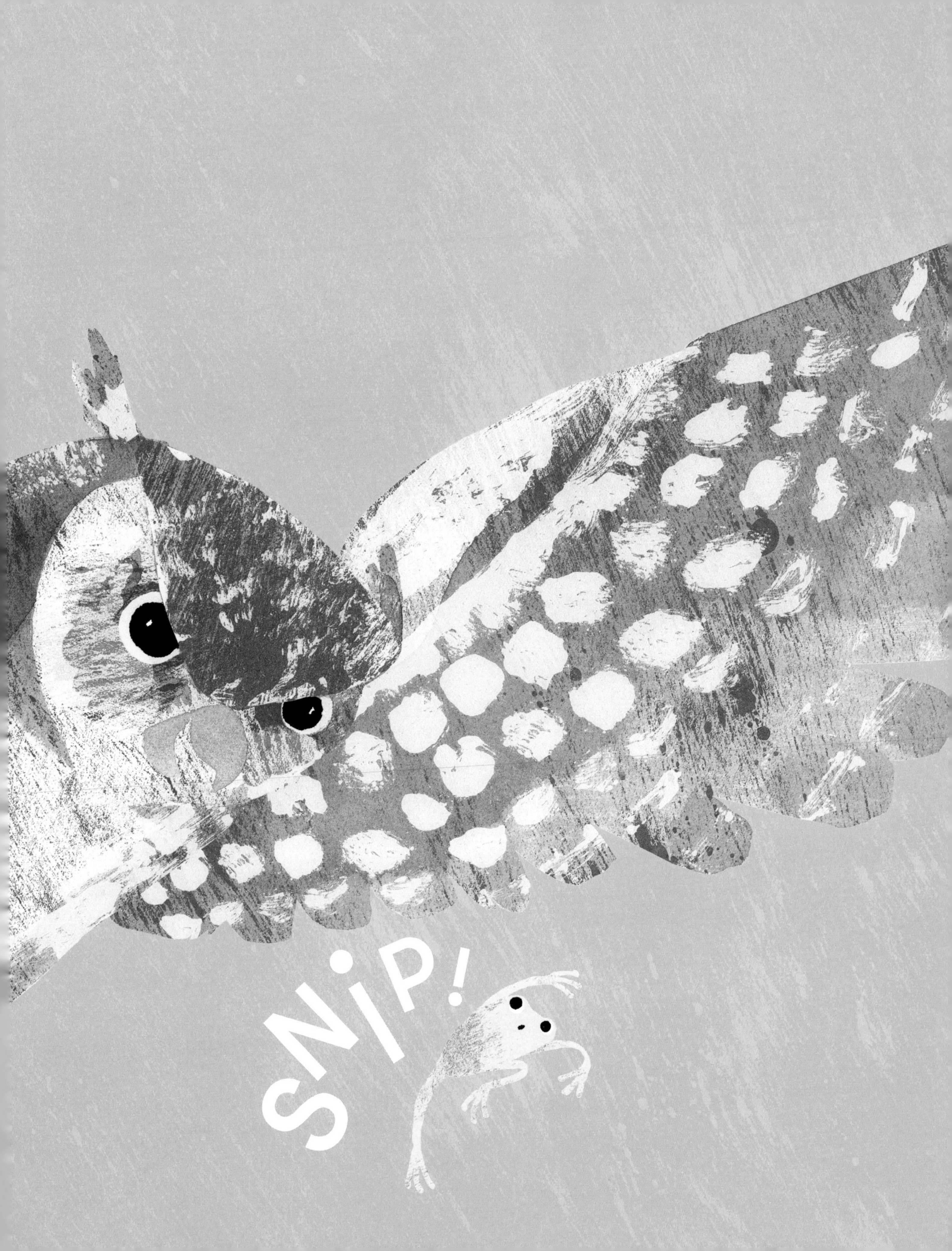
SNIP!

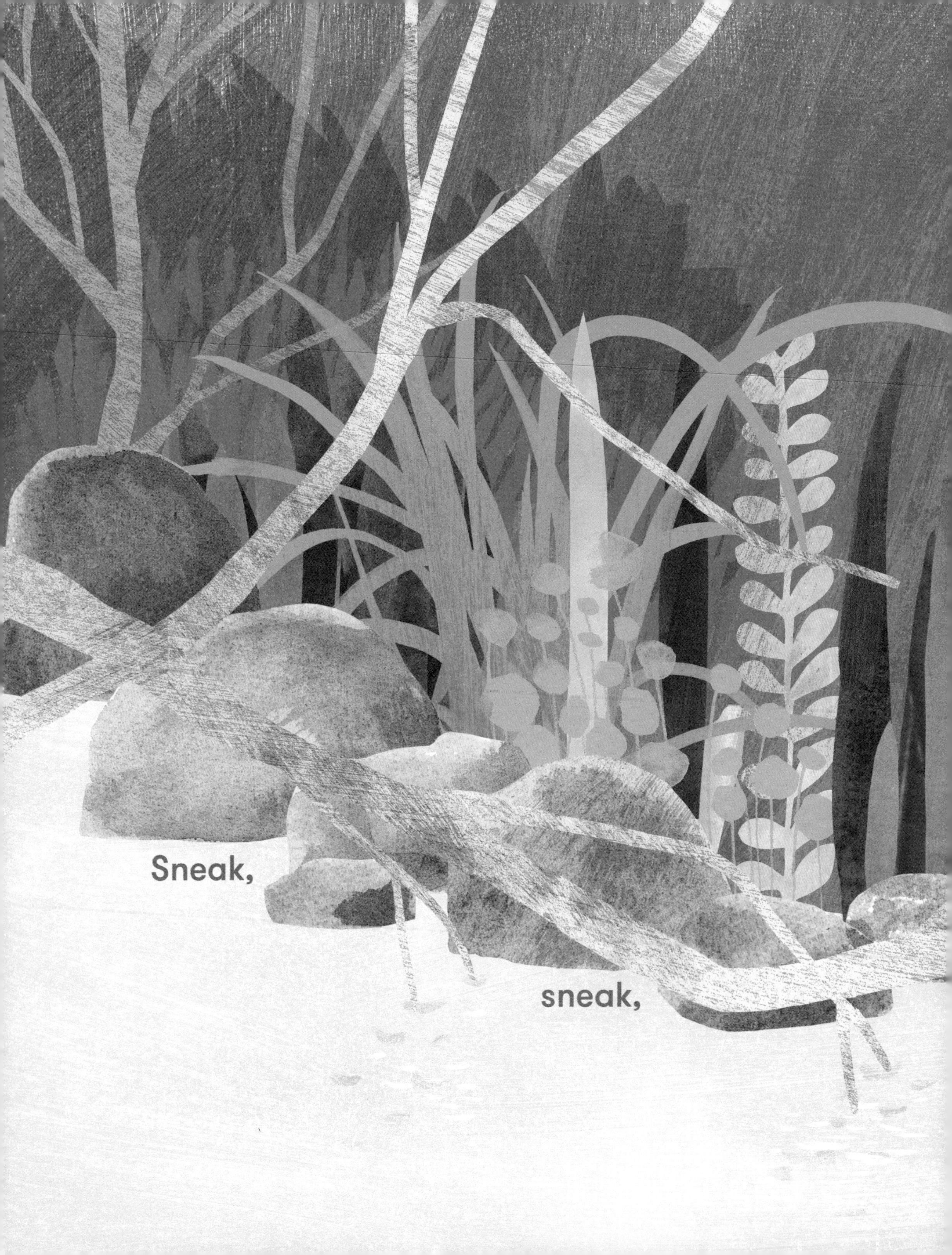

Sneak,

sneak,

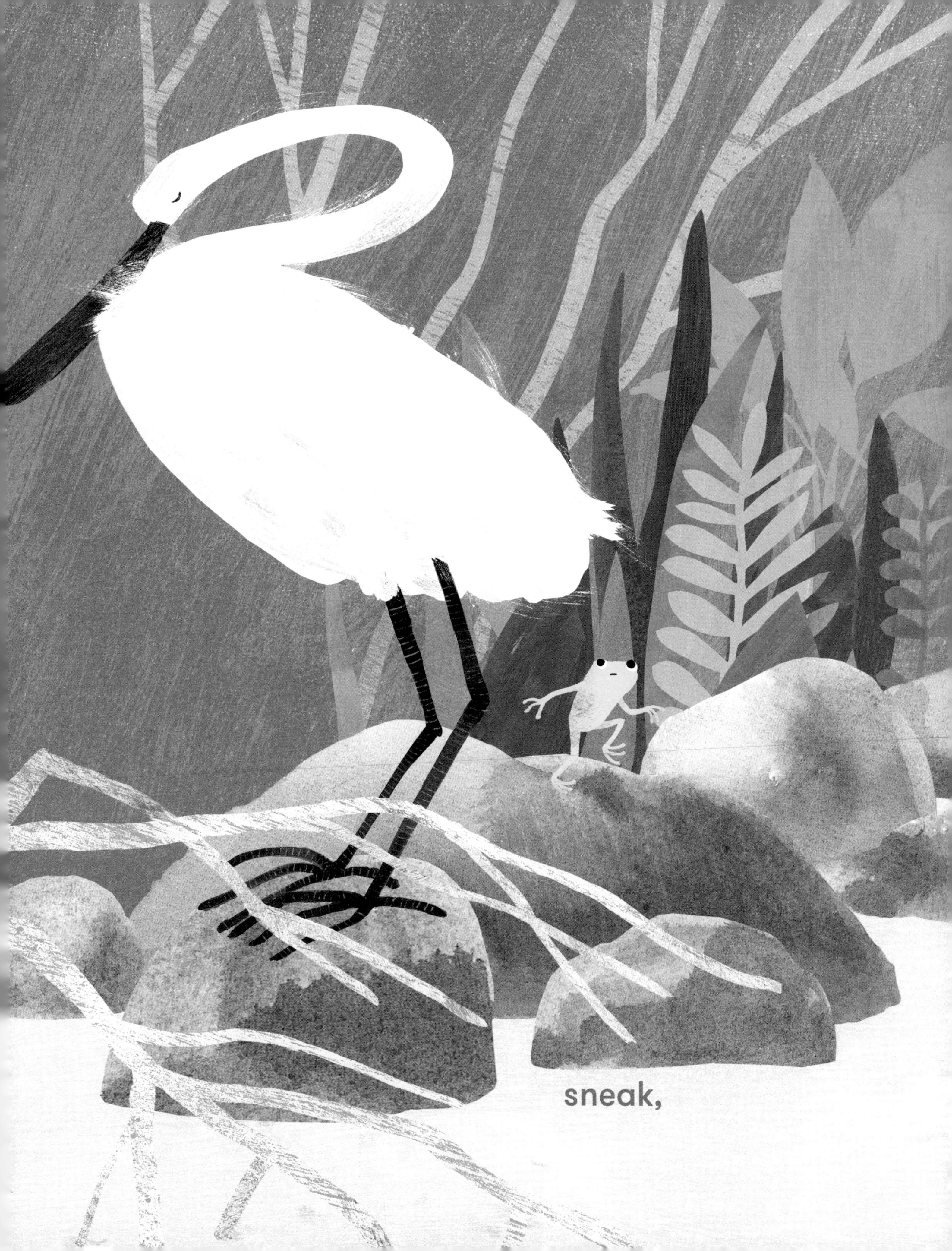

sneak,

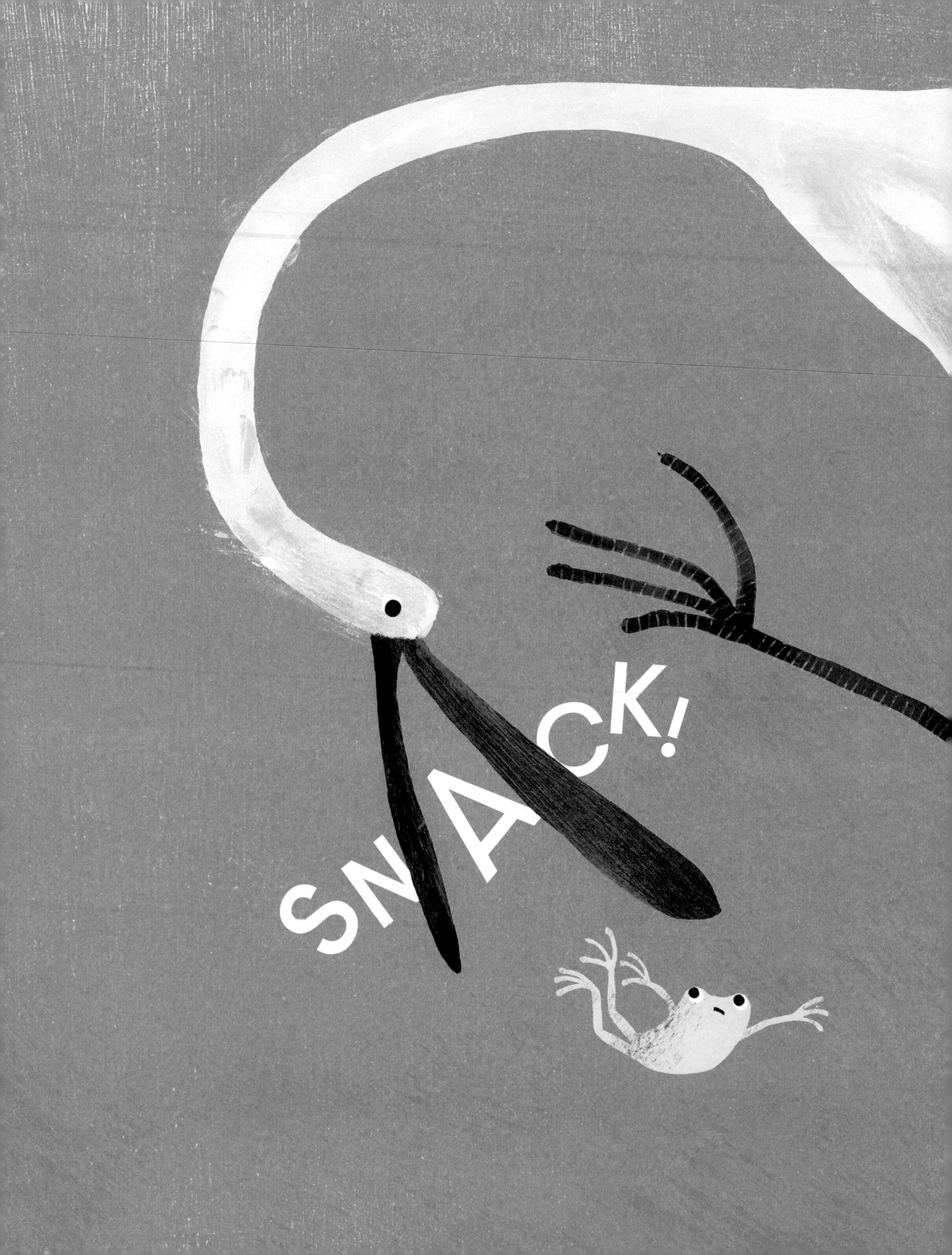
SNACK!

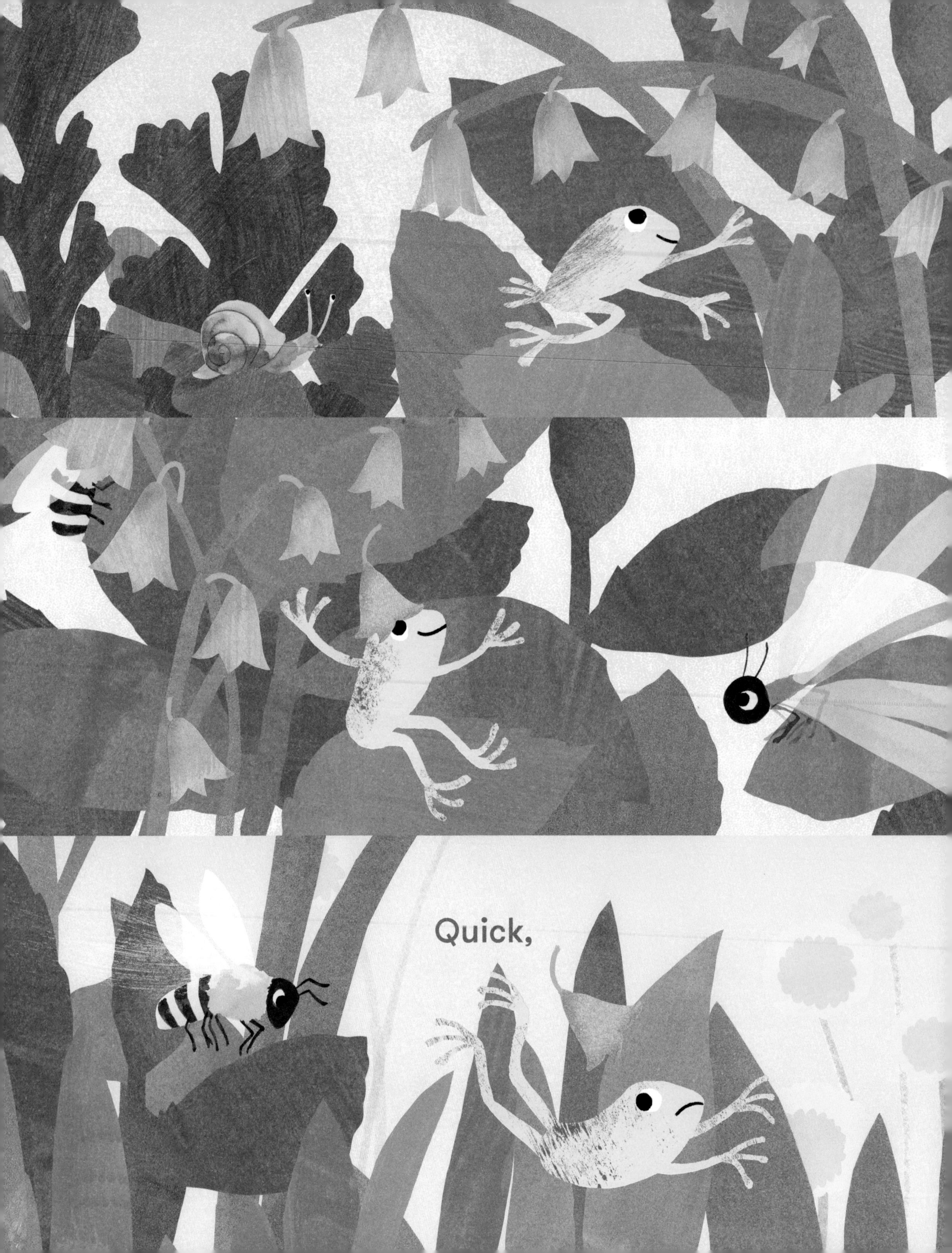
Quick,

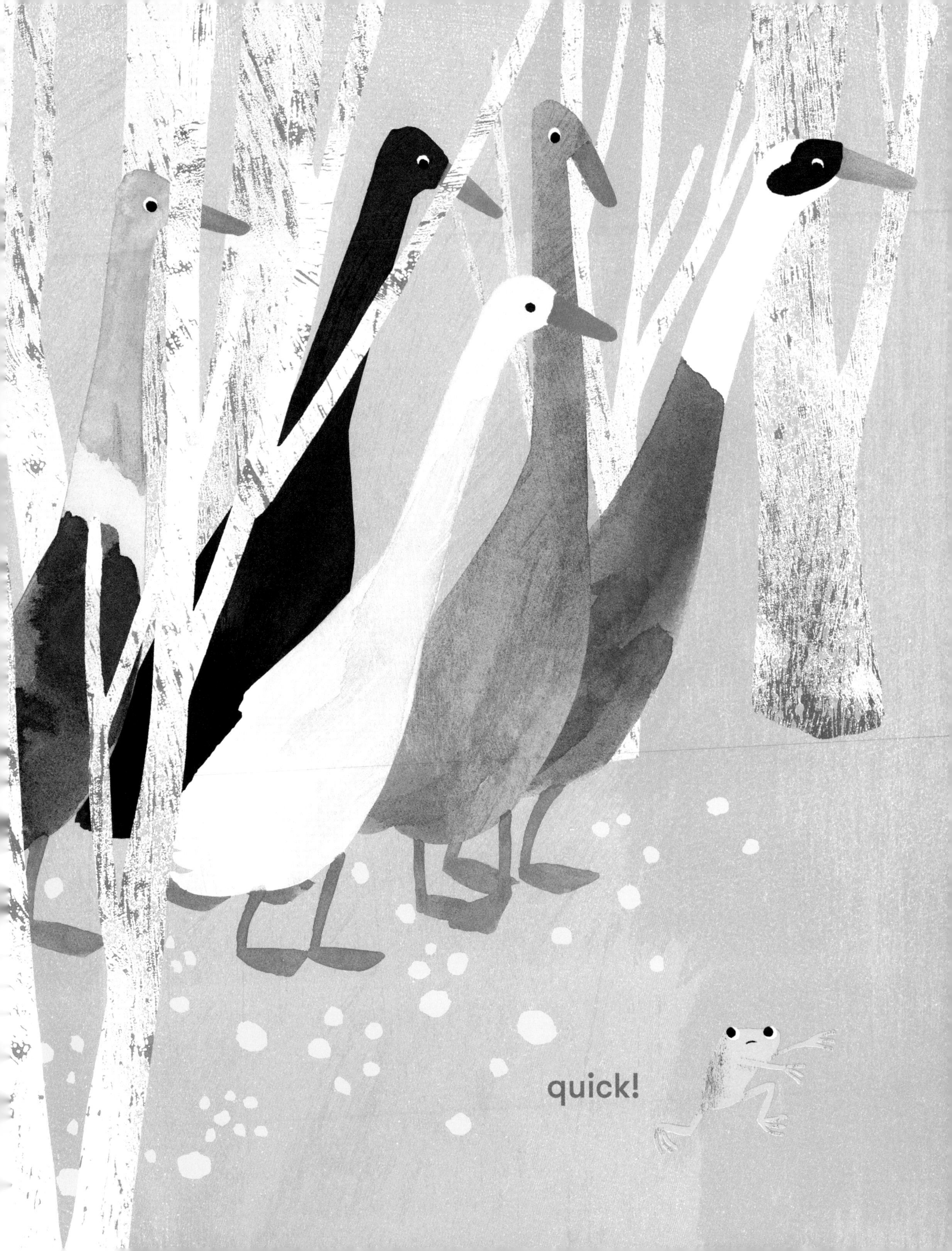

quick!

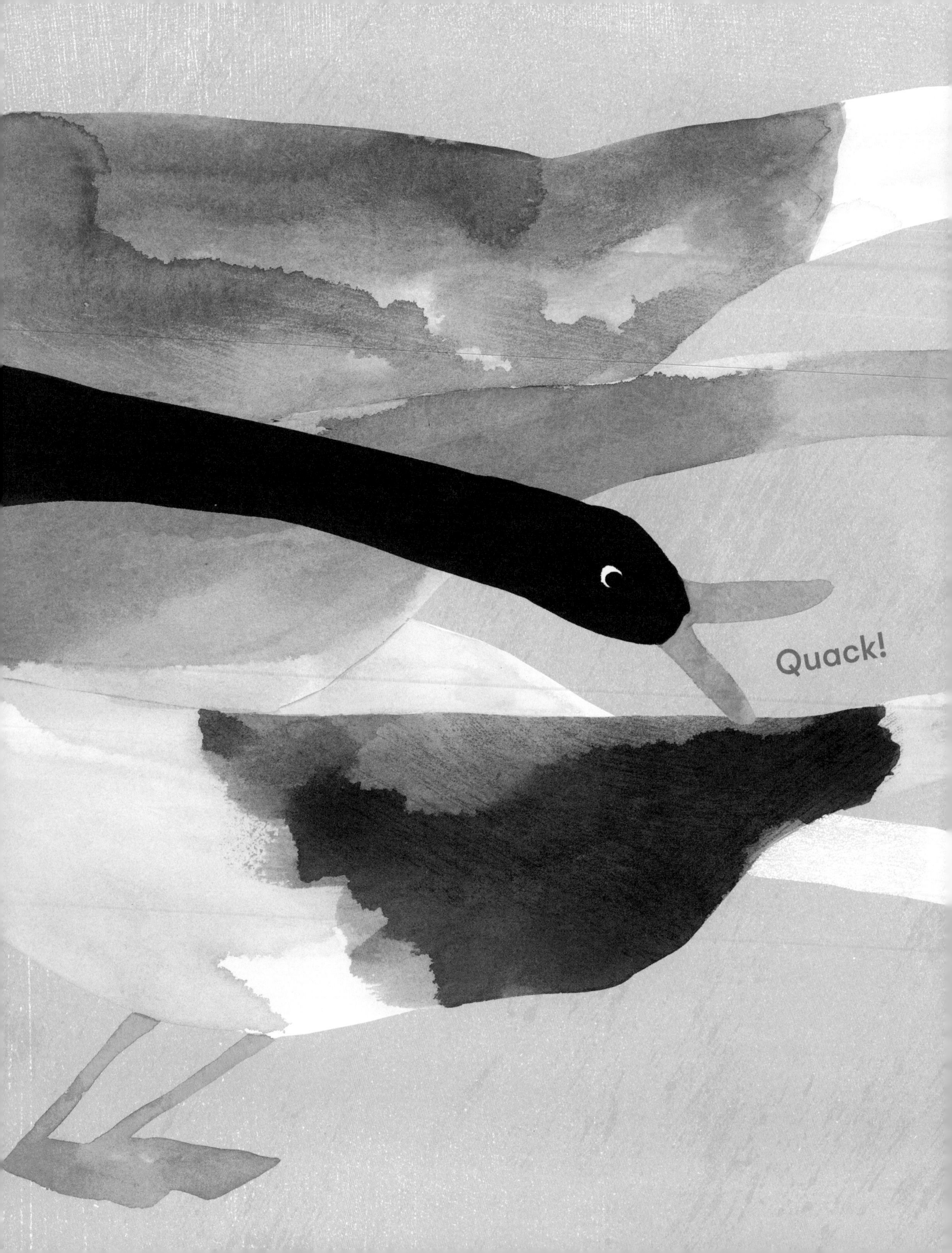
Quack!

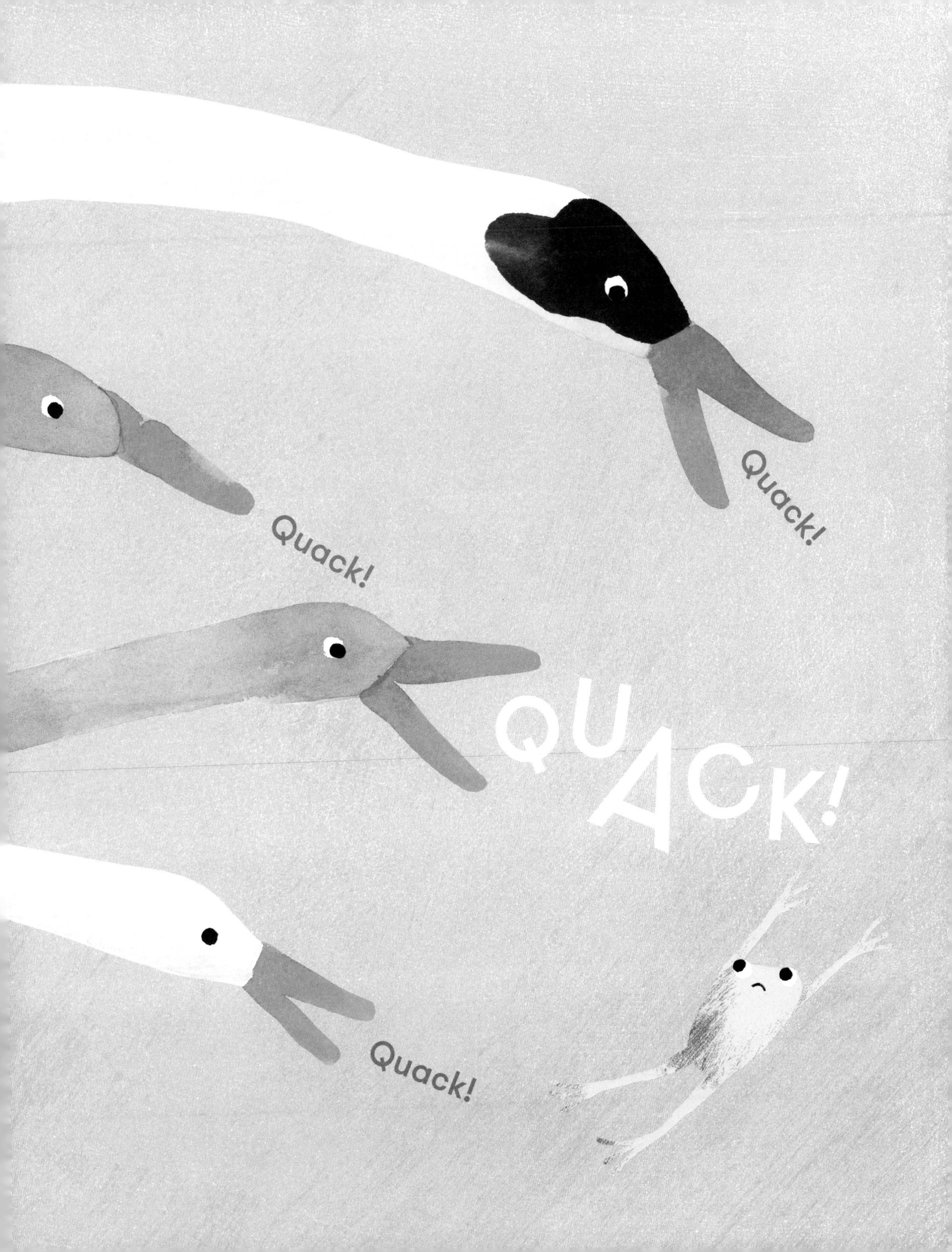
Quack!
Quack!
QUACK!
Quack!

Bump.

Bump.

Jump!

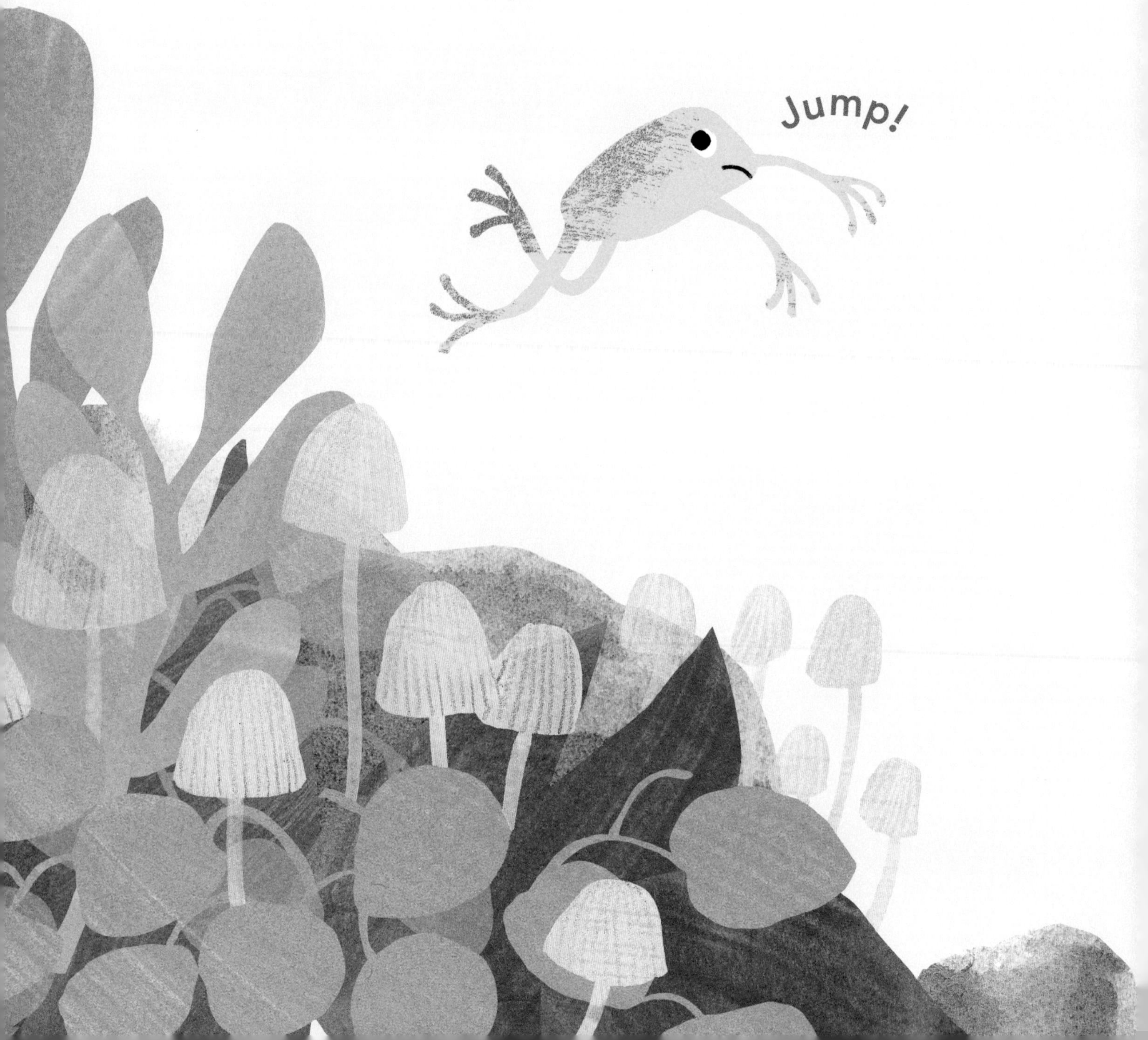

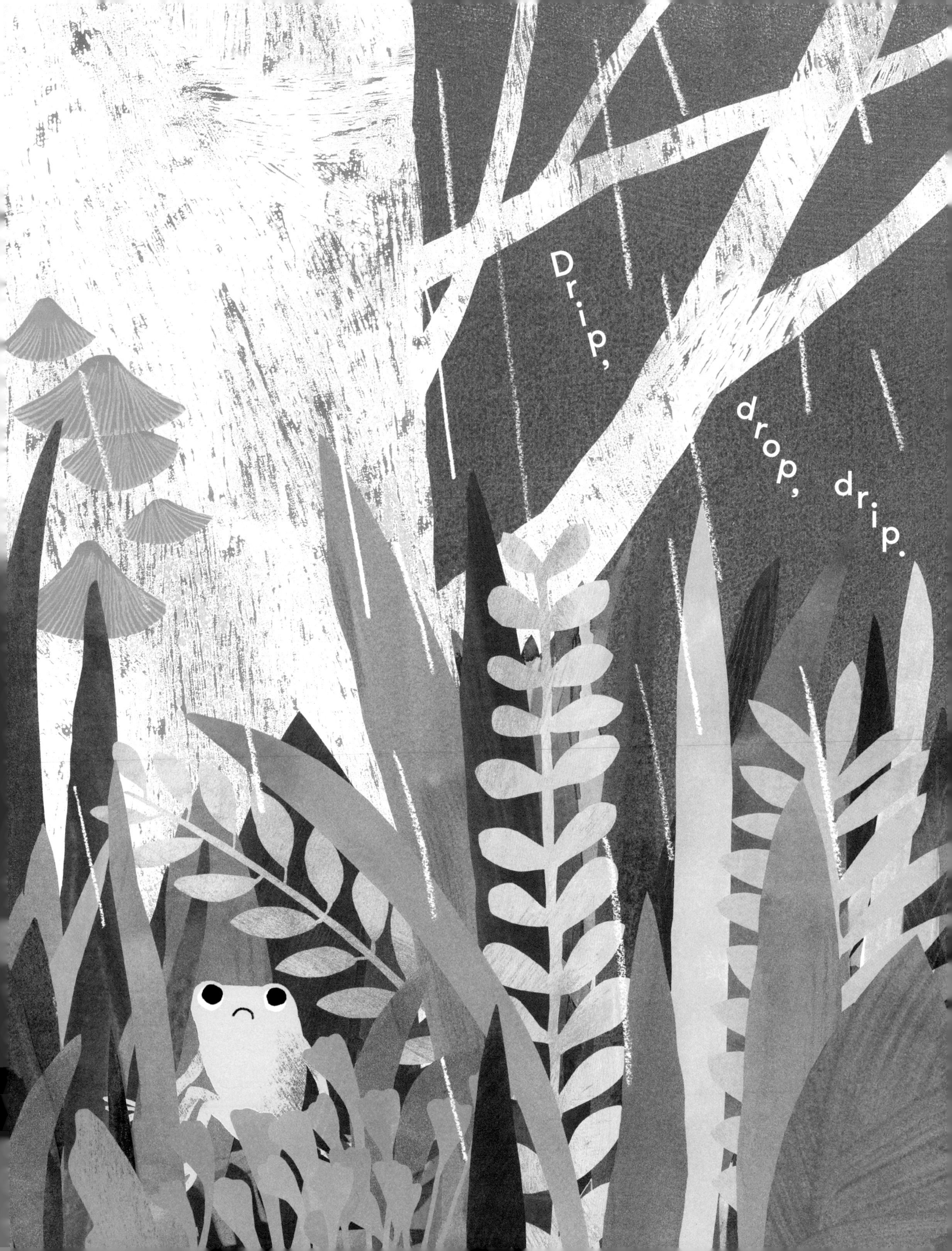

Drip,

drop, drip.

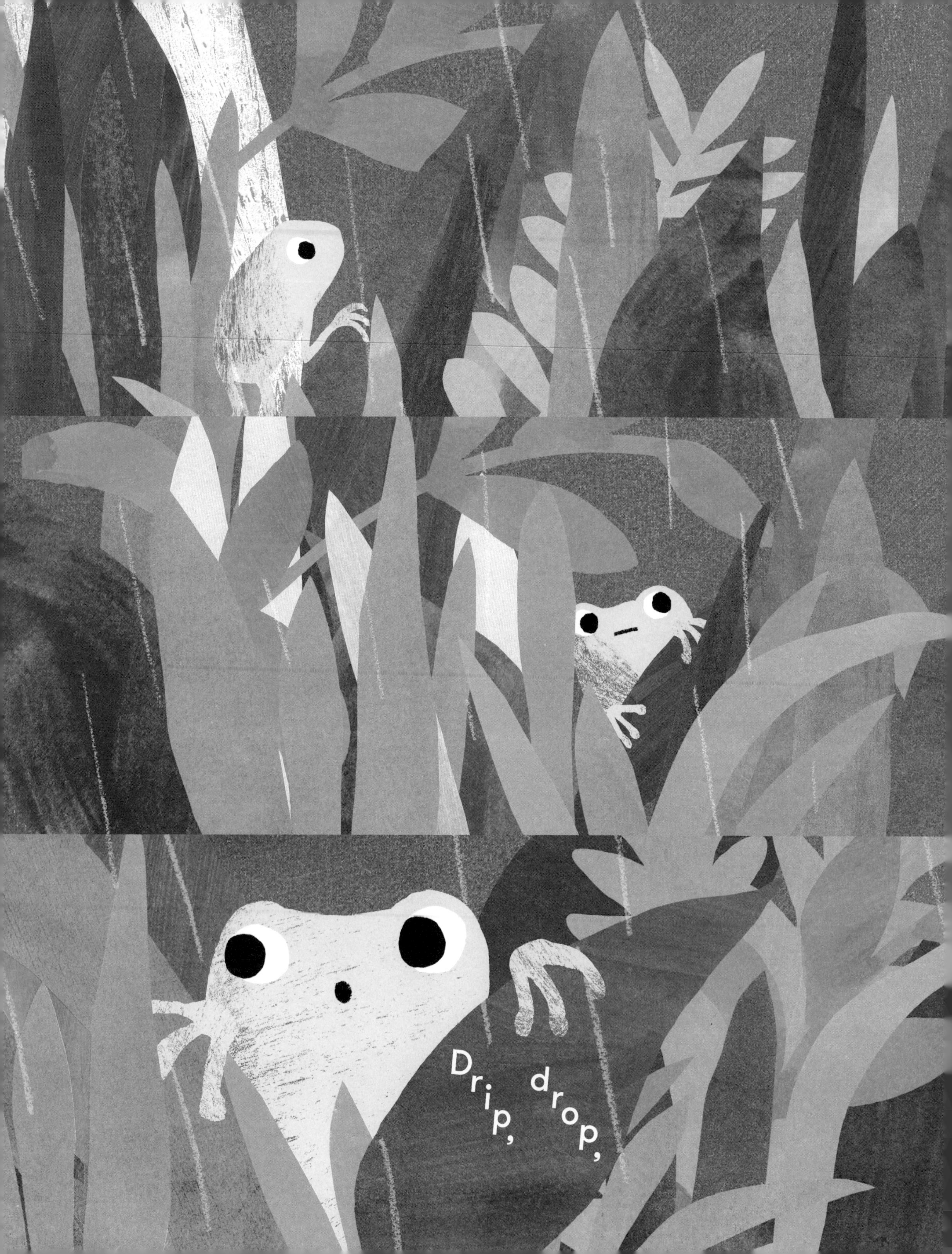
Drip, drop,

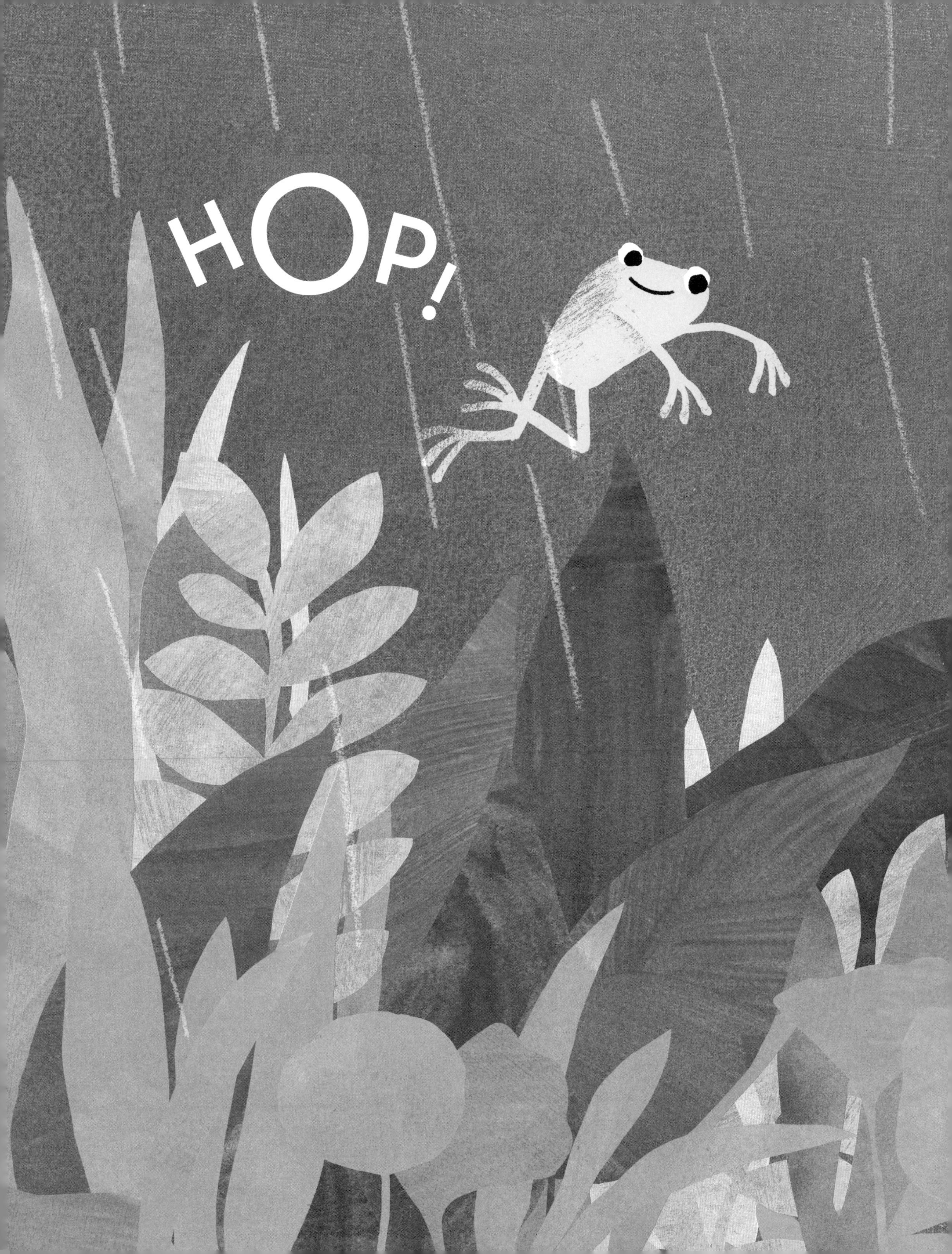
HOP!

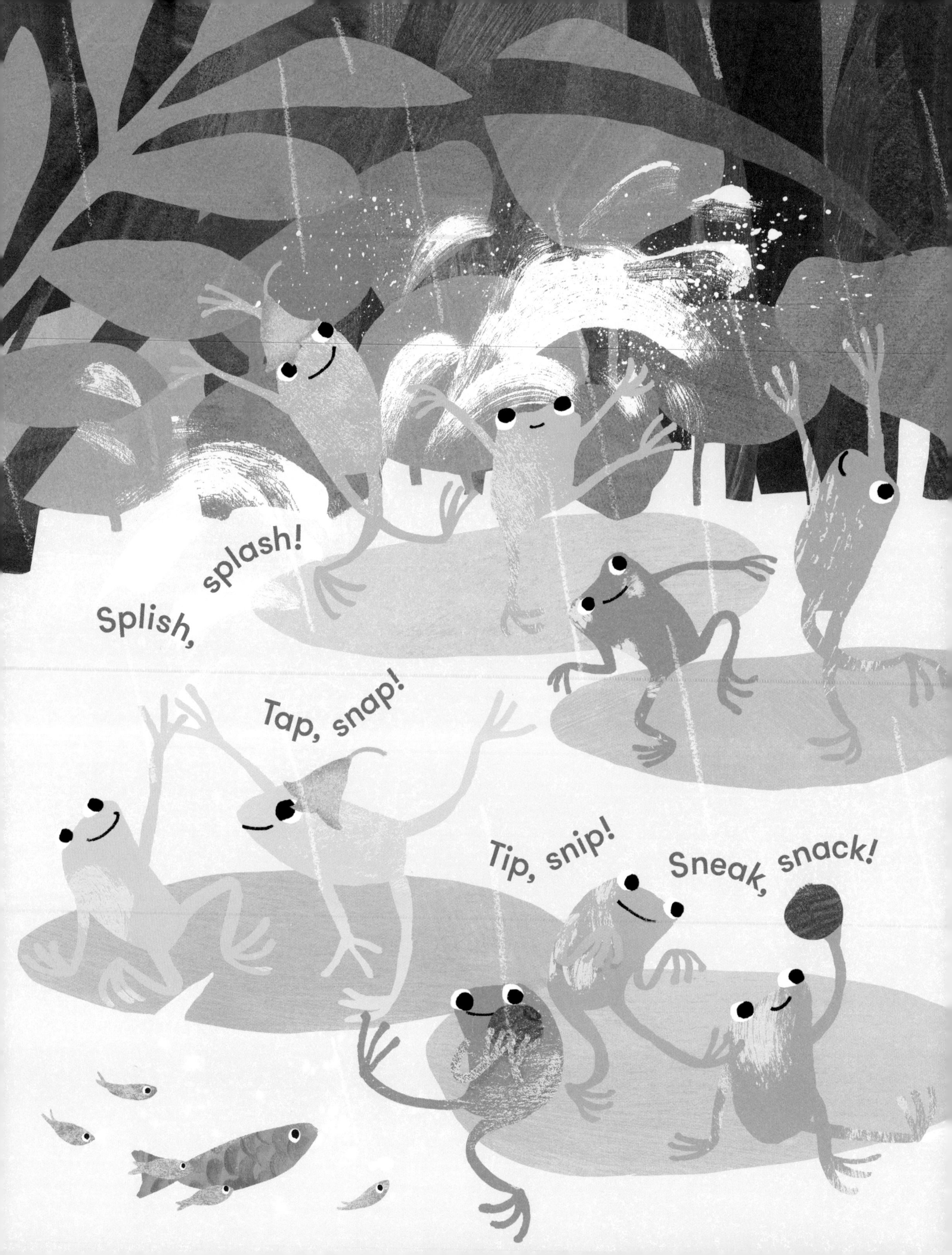

Splish, splash!

Tap, snap!

Tip, snip!

Sneak, snack!

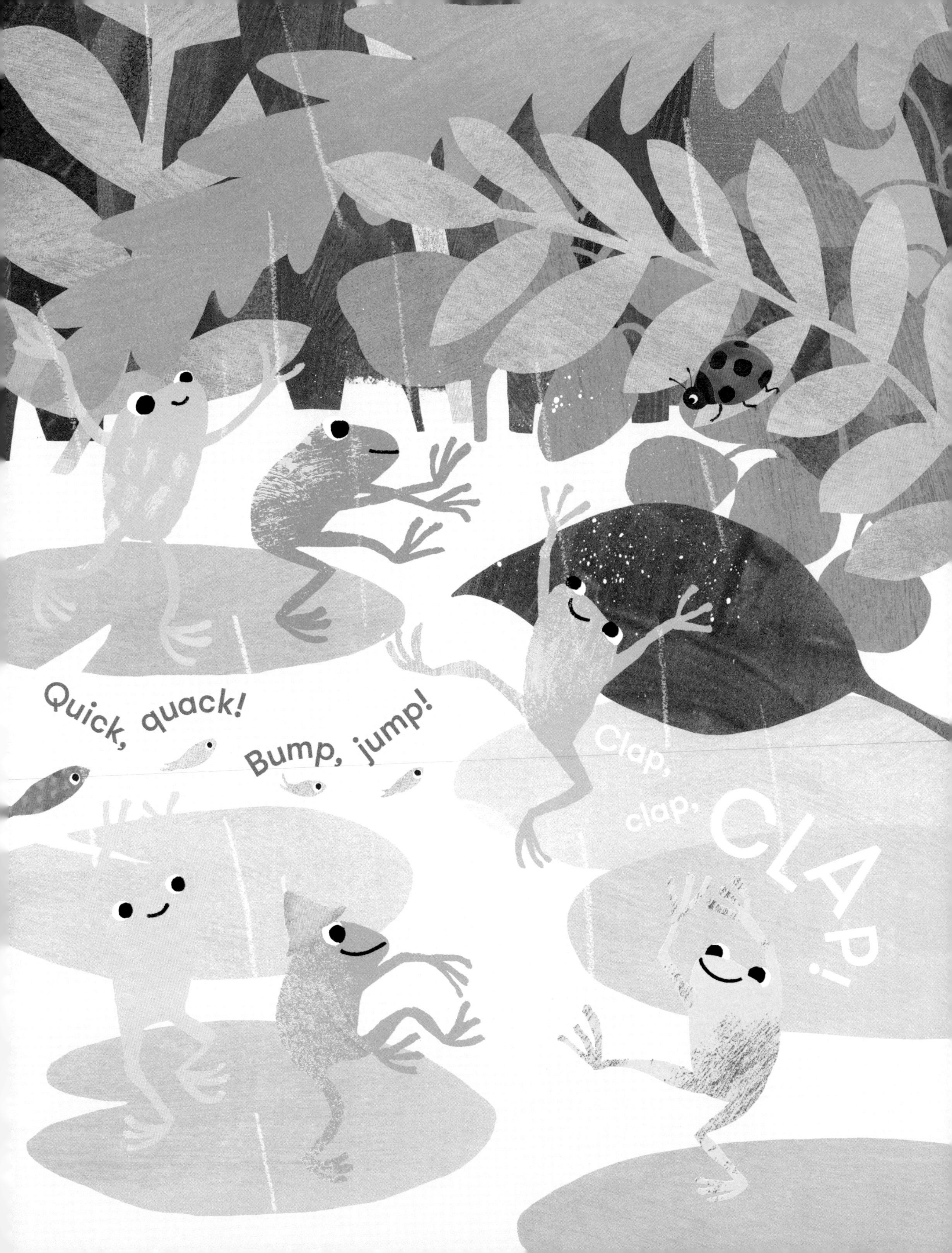
Quick, quack!
Bump, jump!
Clap, clap, CLAP!

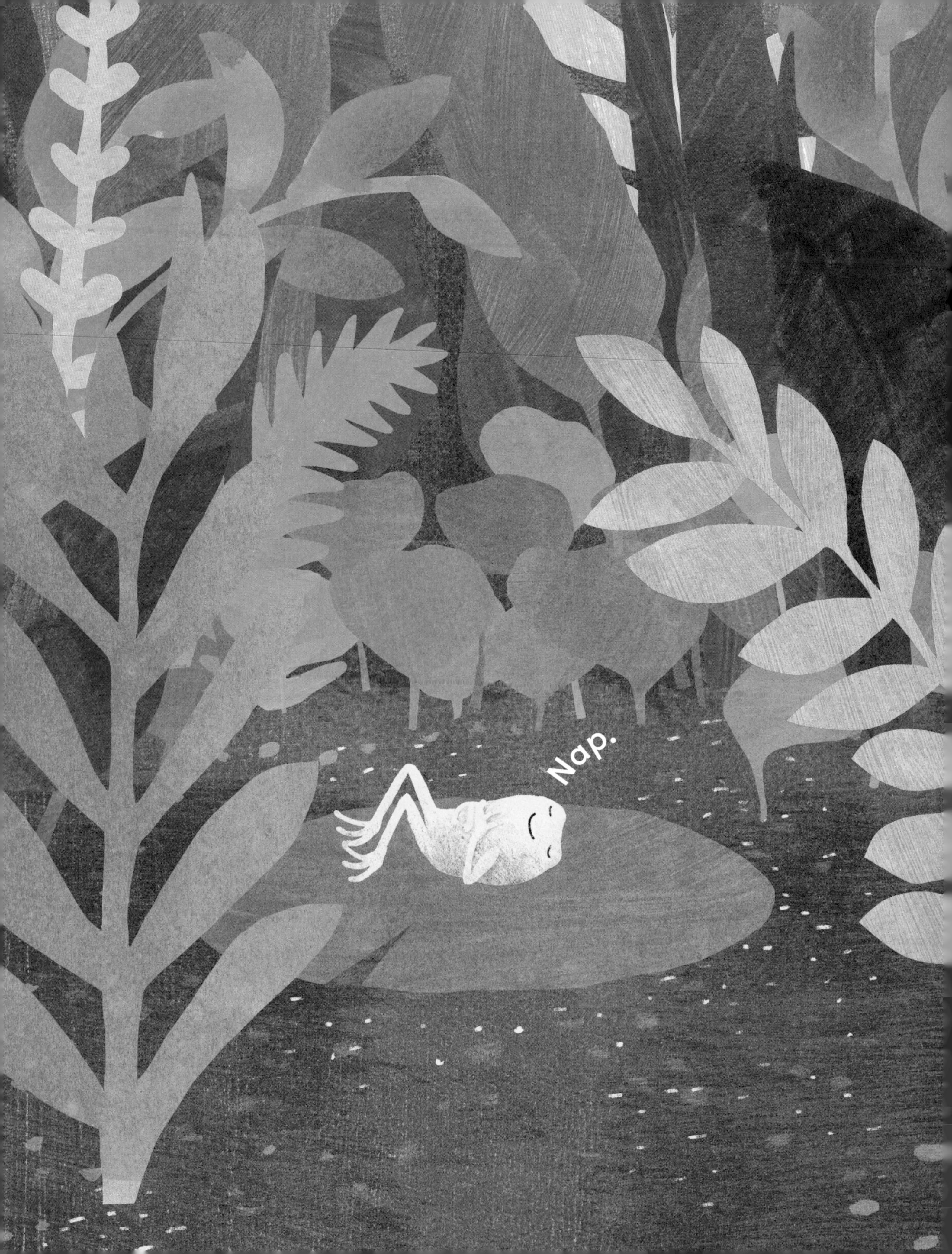
Nap.

The illustrations in this book were created using ink and gouache and digitally assembled.
Typeset in GT Walsheim.

Published by Scribble, an imprint of Scribe Publications, 2022. Reprinted 2023 (twice).
18–20 Edward Street, Brunswick, Victoria 3056, Australia
2 John Street, Clerkenwell, London, WC1N 2ES, United Kingdom
3754 Pleasant Ave, Suite 100, Minneapolis, Minnesota 55409 USA

Design by Miriam Rosenbloom and Guy Ivison.

This book is printed with vegetable-soy based inks, on FSC® certified paper from responsibly managed forests and other controlled material, ensuring that the supply chain from forest to end-user is chain of custody certified.

MIX
Paper | Supporting responsible forestry
FSC® C144853

Printed and bound in China by RR Donnelley.

978 1 922585 38 7 (Australian hardback)
978 1 914484 34 6 (UK hardback)
978 1 957363 24 0 (US hardback)

Catalogue records for this title are available from the National Library of Australia and the British Library.

scribblekidsbooks.com
@scribblekidsbooks

Scribble acknowledges the Wurundjeri Woi Wurrung of the Kulin Nations — the first and continuing custodians of the land on which our books are created. Sovereignty has never been ceded. We pay our respects to Elders past and present.

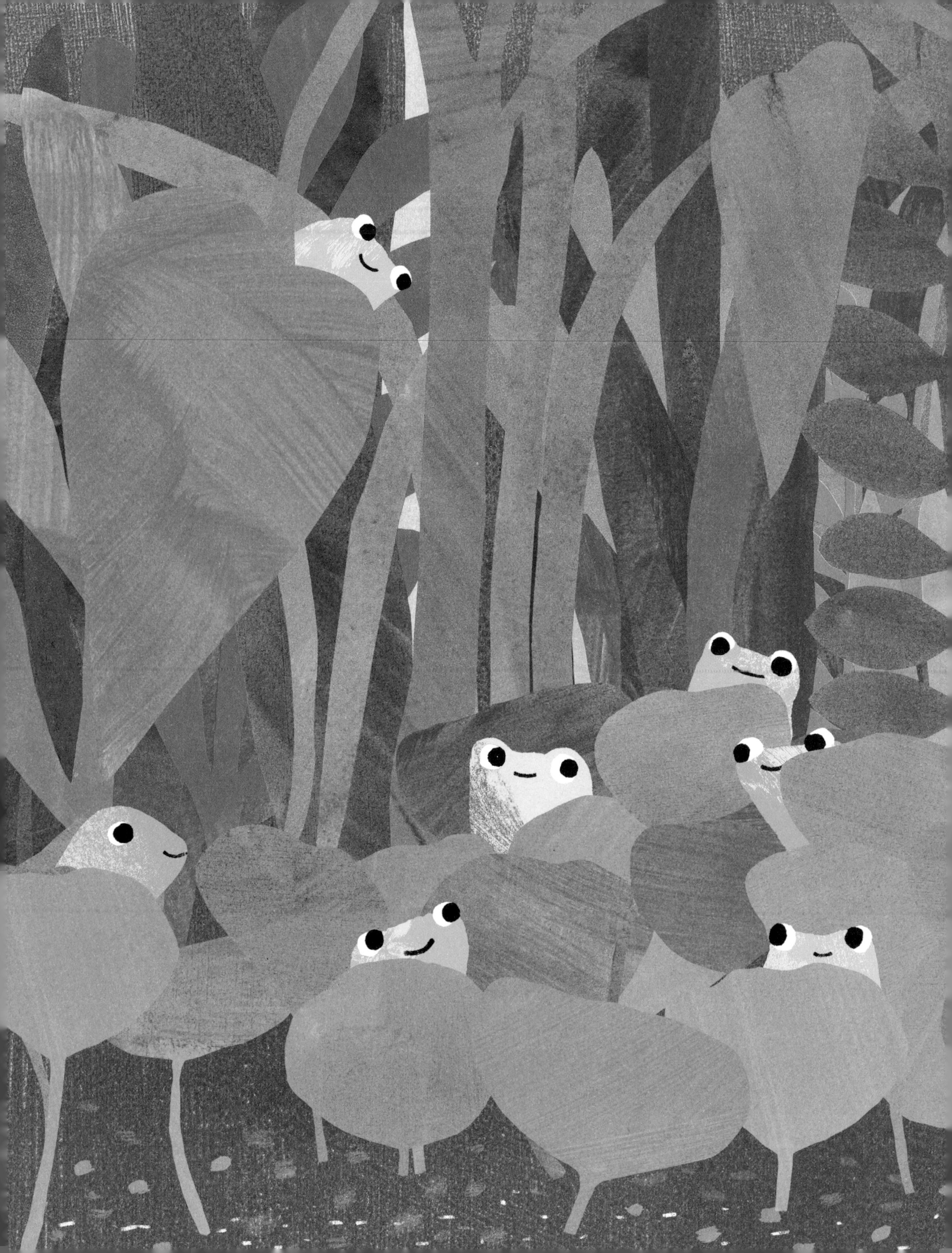

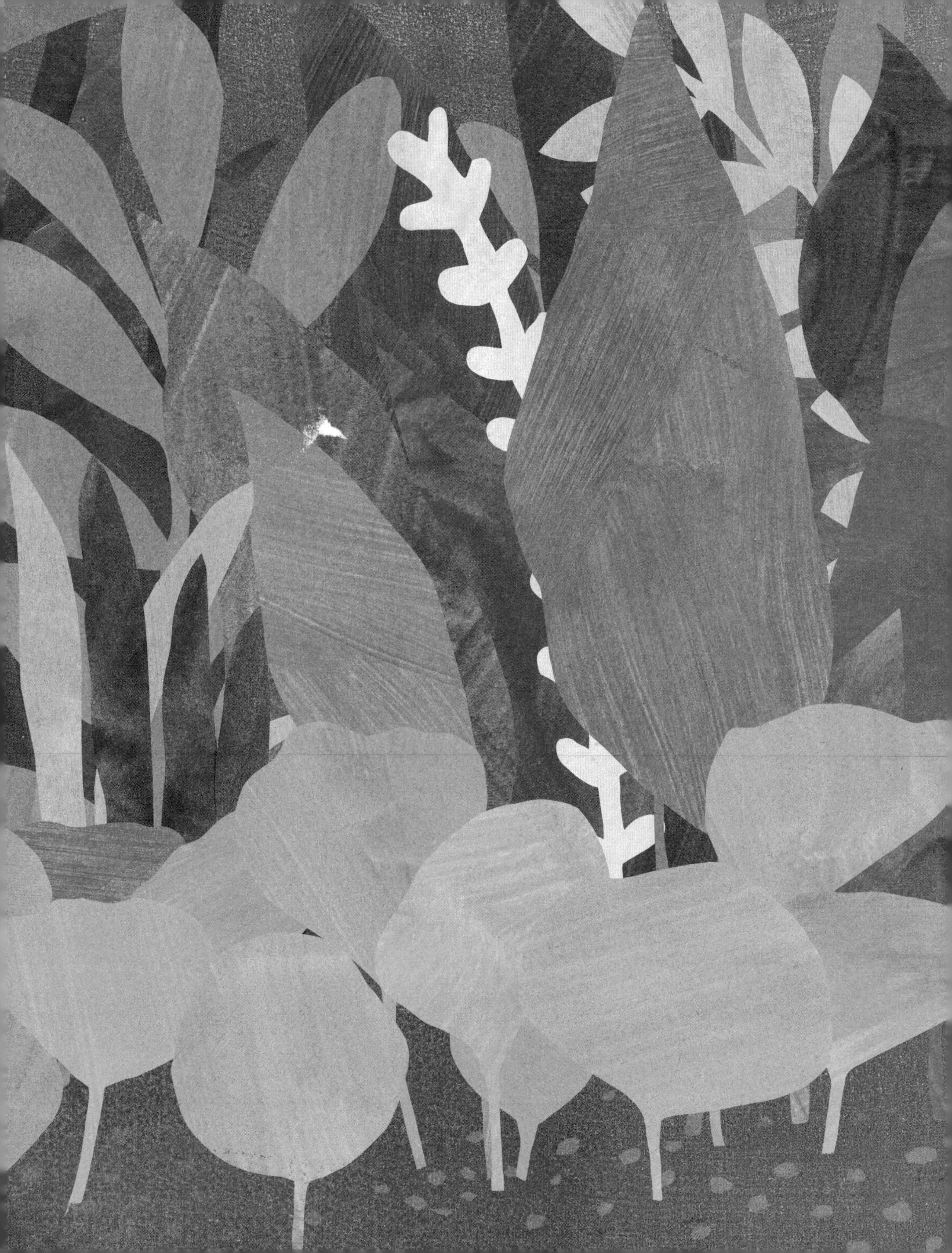

For my studio: Kat, Klarissa, Hamish, and Shelley.